"You haven't been in love," Charles said.

"Most of you city dwellers have emotions that skim lightly over the surface."

He had come too close to her now for comfort and Laraine stood up in a state of panic. "For someone who lives so far away from city dwellers you know a lot about them. If some girl once let you down, don't take it out on me—"

Before she could move he had swept her into his arms. His lips on hers were firm, ruthless and demanding.

Life with Harvey had been like drifting on a quiet lake. In Charles's arms, the emotion she now knew as love, was not a bit like that. It was a raging, relentless current that swept her frighteningly along....

Other titles by
KATRINA BRITT
IN HARLEQUIN ROMANCES

Other titles by
KATRINA BRITT
IN HARLEQUIN PRESENTS

Many of these titles are available at your local bookseller
or through the Harlequin Reader Service.

For a free catalogue listing all available Harlequin Romances,
send your name and address to:

HARLEQUIN READER SERVICE,
M.P.O. Box 707, Niagara Falls, N.Y. 14302
Canadian address: Stratford, Ontario, Canada N5A 6W2

or use coupon at back of book.

Open Not the Door

by

KATRINA BRITT

Harlequin Books

TORONTO • LONDON • NEW YORK • AMSTERDAM
SYDNEY • HAMBURG • PARIS

Original hardcover edition published in 1978
by Mills & Boon Limited

ISBN 0-373-02212-3

Harlequin edition published November 1978

CHAPTER ONE

LARAINE snapped the clasp of her dressing case with a decisive click, and placed it down beside her suitcase on the floor. A sense of anti-climax hovered at the thought of the ordeal ahead. Bracing herself to meet Harvey had taken some courage, but it had to be done, and it was cowardly to send a letter.

Waiting for him to arrive was the worst part. If only she could love him, if only the accident had not happened, if only ... But she did not love Harvey, at least, not in the way her parents had loved each other. Clasping her hands in front of her, Laraine stared down at her luggage through a mist of tears. She thought of her happy childhood with her parents before her mother had died and her father had gone abroad. She remembered receiving news of his death from a motoring accident while covering a story for his paper, and putting all she had into her first typing job after leaving college. At the age of eighteen her world had crashed. Now she was twenty-four and still alone.

It was not that she was cold or very selective where the opposite sex was concerned, it was simply that the right man had not come along. She would know him when he did. The boys who had dated her had been nice, young and wholesome—more or less out of the same mould in the way that not one of them stirred her into a deeper feeling than that of friendship. Like Harvey.

They had met at the wedding of her best friend, Jane Myott, in fashionable Knightsbridge. Jane, a secretary, had married her boss, an executive; a young man who had reached the top at the age of thirty by sheer ability. Robert Tate was an attractive man with a conservative taste in dress, but Laraine had thought him too full of his own importance and a bore.

Harvey, on the other hand, was reserved and rather dull. He was a successful speculator who had also done well on the Stock Exchange, but his business acumen did not help in his relationships with women.

Jane had said, 'I don't know why Robert and Harvey are such good friends. They're not alike in any way except that they're both successful in their own particular field. Harvey is only twenty-eight and looks older. Anyway, he's to be best man and will pair off beautifully with my chief brides-maid, my darling Laraine. Be nice to him, pet. I have high hopes for you two. Think how wonderful it would be if you were to make a match of it! Can you imagine both of us with a house in the executive belt and our children going to the same kind of school?'

Laraine had laughed. Like Harvey and Robert, Jane had little in common with herself. To be married to a success-ful man, to have his family and mix with what she called the right people, had been the be-all and end-all to Jane. But Laraine was different. Material things were the last on her list. She wanted to be loved for herself and needed. When the right man came along it would not matter if he had not a penny as long as they loved each other. Maybe Jane, being an orphan too, had wanted security for me, Laraine had thought, maybe she had thought that since my dates with men had come to nothing I too was waiting for a successful Robert Tate or Harvey Strang.

At the wedding reception, Harvey had sat next to her, a thick-set young man of medium height, not bad-looking but obviously no ladies' man. Laraine had been surprised to find that pity for him had aroused a friendly feeling in her warm heart and it showed in her lovely smile.

'I hate tomatoes. I wonder, would you ...?' she had whispered, quelling a shudder at the lobster and prawn salad on her plate decorated with artistically cut tomatoes. 'I know it isn't the thing, but if you're quick...'

So Harvey had obliged by whipping the offending toma-toes on to his plate.

From then on it had been plain sailing between them. He

told her that he was having trouble getting a good secretary since his had left to get married, and Laraine had sympathised, since she was a secretary herself to a very nice business man in the city.

When finally Jane, exquisite in her going away outfit of pale blue, had floated away in heavenly bliss on the first stage of her honeymoon, Harvey was completely relaxed. The wedding reception had continued for the rest of the afternoon and evening with the guests dancing to a good band in the exclusive hotel rooms hired for the occasion.

Laraine had enjoyed it. Harvey danced fairly well and was full of apologies for his amateur performance, confessing that he had lost touch with social events for a long time, but he planned on altering that. She had not asked him how he planned to alter things and had pleaded another engagement when later he had taken her back to her flat and suggested they met again.

For a while after Harvey had said it with flowers, with a bouquet arriving at her flat every morning in between telephone calls. He was still trying to arrange a date when Jane arrived back from her honeymoon, and they met again at Jane's house-warming party in her new home.

'Be nice to Harvey, Laraine,' she had pleaded. 'The poor soul has led such a dull life making money. He's very smitten with you, and you could have him like a shot. He can't get over the fact that he feels so relaxed and happy in your company.'

By the end of the year she was going out with him and had become more than skilful in refusing the many gifts of jewellery and furs which he was so eager to shower upon her. She would have been less than human not to derive a certain amount of enjoyment by being taken around by a wealthy man, but she did insist upon keeping their friendship platonic.

They had been to dinner with Jane and Robert to discuss plans for a summer holiday together on Harvey's yacht, and were returning for Harvey to drop her at her flat when the accident happened. They had hardly left Jane's house when Harvey had asked her to marry him. Laraine had refused as gently as she could, reminding him that she had never given him any false hopes in that direction. Too late she had seen her mistake in telling him while he was driving the car. He was very upset, and Laraine recalled the extra drinks he had taken earlier that evening at dinner, no doubt to bolster up his courage to propose.

His hands holding the wheel had been shaking and it was evident that he had been very upset. He was going far too quick on approaching the blind corner and the blue Mini had taken the turn too wide. Laraine shivered to see Harvey's big car toss it aside into a spin. The driver, a girl, had been thrown out but had not been killed.

Harvey and she had escaped injury thanks to their seat belts, and he had got off lightly since the driver of the Mini had come out on her wrong side. The alcohol in his blood had slightly exceeded the limit, but he had gone through all the tests and no charge had been made. The matter had been settled out of court, with Harvey paying up handsomely to the driver of the Mini.

Laraine was shaken abruptly out of her thoughts at the sound of a car braking in the street below her open window. Trembling a little, she reached out for the topcoat, handbag and gloves on her bed. Then with a last look round the flat that had been her home for the past four years, she went downstairs.

Harvey was just leaving the big luxurious car when she reached the street. He was wearing his usual expansive smile and gazing appraisingly at her slim, sophisticated smartness in the cream tailored dress with the matching coat carried elegantly over her arm.

'Hello, Harvey.' Laraine lifted a delicate oval face set in an aura of rich dark hair. 'I'm sorry, but I'm not going with you.'

His face turned to a dull red. 'Not coming?' he repeated stupidly.

'That's right. I told you I wasn't the other evening when you asked me to think it over. I've thought it over and the answer is the same. I'm not coming.'

'But you're all ready,' he blustered. 'You can't mean you're still going on with that harebrained scheme of yours? Just because some fool of a girl ran into us and received injuries which were caused by her own carelessness you go all hysterical and want to take care of her...'

Laraine broke in firmly. 'I'm sorry, but my mind is made up.'

Harvey's mouth had dropped open as anger hardened his features. It occurred to Laraine in that moment that he looked almost coarse and even repulsive. His usual likeable genial mask had slipped to show the real Harvey Strang, the ruthless speculator—the self-made, self-indulgent man who thought that money was God. He made an effort to conceal his anger. His voice became soft, coaxing, but the pale blue eyes were as cold as ice.

'Laraine darling,' he began softly, 'you can't let your friends Jane and Robert down like this, not to mention me. They'll be on my yacht by now, waiting for us to join them with a month's cruise in mind. Aren't you being selfish and just a little silly, upsetting us all like this? After all, the girl might resent you reminding her of the accident. Damn it all, she did run into us!'

'I know,' Laraine said quietly. 'But I can't help but think we might have been hurt as badly had we been in a Mini too. The long bonnet of your car and the seat belts saved us from serious injury, whereas that poor girl...'

He cut in savagely, 'That poor girl wasn't wearing her seat belt and she ran into us.' He was fast losing his temper again. 'Come on,' he said roughly, 'we're wasting time.'

'Yes, we are, since I'm not coming with you. Goodbye, Harvey. Have a nice holiday. I've already telephoned for a taxi to take me to the station. I can hardly expect you to take me.'

Harvey exploded at this, causing two small boys who

were playing close by to pause in their game and stare wide-eyed in their direction.

He ignored them. 'Like hell I will!' he roared. 'What do you take me for? Why, there are hundreds of girls much prettier than you who'd give anything for a month's cruise on a yacht. You little fool!'

By now Laraine was staring at him as wide-eyed as the two small boys as he implied so forcibly all that she was throwing away. But with a sense of shock she knew that she was throwing nothing away by parting company with a man who might have made her miserable for the rest of her life. It was with a sense of relief that she held out her hand.

'I'm sorry, Harvey,' she said. 'Goodbye.'

But Harvey was too furious to take her outstretched hand. He swung round on a venomous look, flung himself into his car, and drove away at speed. She was still staring after him when her taxi arrived.

The express squeaked to a halt and a confusion of sound echoed in the cavernous roof of the station as porters shouted, doors were opened and trolleys rattled. Laraine stepped down on to the platform and tried to take it in that she was here in Scotland, where it seemed that all the passengers leaving the train were being met with the exception of herself.

Her heart began to pound the colour to her cheeks as she looked around with apprehension for someone who would come forward and make himself known. Eventually the crowd thinned and she found herself alone with her cases beside her and not a porter in sight. She turned and looked hopefully towards the barrier where the ticket collector was waiting and found herself trembling with an urge to turn around and rush back to the train before it left the station.

'Excuse me.'

Someone was suddenly towering above her. Somewhat startled, Laraine blinked and looked up into his face. His height and breadth of shoulder blotted out the surroundings. He had spoken cultured English, and his sudden appearance filled her with a spurious excitement at the unexpected. His fair hair and blue eyes reminded her of a Nordic king, and she did like the blue tartan tam-o'-shanter topped by a brown bob set flat on the thick fair hair. It occurred to her that one could call him good-looking in a strong-boned arrogant way. Smiling at him, Laraine felt for some idiotic reason that she wanted to go on doing so.

But he was not smiling at all. Indeed, he gave the impression that he was approaching her because he had been requested to do so. This he confirmed in his deep pleasing voice.

Unsmiling, he said, 'You must be Miss Laraine Winters. I'm Charles McGreyfarne. I was asked to pick you up since I was passing this way. Is this all your luggage?'

Laraine nodded, and without giving her time to speak, he was picking it up with effortless ease to stride towards the barrier. Laraine tendered her ticket before hastening after him, noting as she did so the impeccable cut of his breeches and riding jacket. The latter fitted his wide shoulders with a military smartness which suggested a latent quality of hidden strength. There was a kind of indolent grace about him as he reached the horsebox and shoved the luggage in the back before letting the door down. For an instant Laraine was again taken aback. A horsebox? The man had probably just returned from taking a horse somewhere, since it was empty.

She wondered who he was and why he was so impersonal, almost rude in his abruptness. Keen eagle eyes in a healthy bronzed face caught and held her own as he moved around to open the door of the cab for her. There was no pleasure kindling there, and a sense of coldness shot through her. He helped her in and slipped in behind the wheel. Laraine had felt herself held by that gaze, deep, probing, and disturbingly so. The warm colour had rushed to her face, and she lowered her head to hide her confusion as she got into the cab.

It was the first time she had found a man's gaze so significant, so overwhelming. No man had ever looked at her in that way before and she resented it—so much so that as he put on speed she was able to look at him with cool composure. The deceptively light touch of his firm brown hands on the wheel hinted at the subtle charm of his personality, a swift withdrawal from any close contact with his passenger, the relaxed poise of his body showing an alert brain.

How old was he? she asked herself ... twenty-seven, twenty-eight? He had the look of a mature man of experience. That firm determined jawline above the polo neck of his cream sweater and that well cut mouth which could, if he let it, curve up at the corners, and that long masculine nose had all the hallmarks of a ladykiller. She could see him tossing a caber at the Highland Games and treading the light fantastic with some bonny Scots lass, as much at home on the dance floor as on the sports ground.

They had left the brown, pine-needled track twisting through sun-dappled trees from the station to speed along a freshly surfaced road between hedgerows of burgeoning white candy-floss hawthorn. On either side the hills were bright with gorse, and a lone heron winged overhead. Laraine sat up as rolling meadows thick with wild grasses and thistle became dotted with cattle, unfamiliar white beasts.

'What beautiful cattle!' she cried. 'And all white. How very extraordinary!'

He tossed a glance at her lively interest. Her cheeks were slightly flushed, her eyes bright, and her pink lips slightly parted to show small, white, even teeth. The gleam of interest in his eyes could be a trick of the light.

He smiled, a slow charming smile tilting up the corners of his mouth as she imagined it would. Her heart tilted.

'Chillingham cattle,' he said. 'And not a black sheep in sight. They descend from the white oxen which roamed the forests of North Britain several hundred years ago. Fantastic, isn't it, that they've never been known to produce a coloured or even partly coloured offspring?'

'They're very beautiful,' she said. 'You sounded a trifle sardonic when you mentioned black sheep. Are you one?'

He lifted a brow as he set the car towards the hills.

'No. Sorry to disappoint you,' he drawled laconically.

She flashed him an indignant look from stormy brown eyes. 'Why should I be disappointed? I don't know you, so I don't have feelings about you one way or the other. You, it seems, have little time for me. I wonder why you came. After all, I could have hired a taxi and enjoyed the drive.'

She gripped her hands tightly in her lap. If the girl she was proposing to look after was as unpleasant as he was, her plans would certainly have to be revised. He did not answer but seemed to be concentrating on the road ahead. It was then that she saw the slow-moving little brown object in the centre of the road, and he seemed to be making straight for it. Even as the hedgehog closed itself up into a ball, Laraine closed her eyes, and clenched her hands.

She felt the van move to the side of the road and stop. His door clicked open and he shot her a sardonic glance.

'Like to come for a small stroll?' he asked.

His voice was courteous, and lacking in warmth as Laraine opened her eyes. Too late she wished that an interview between herself and her future employer had been fixed to give her some idea what kind of treatment to expect. Surely the girl did not doubt her sincerity in wanting to help? Anyway, much as she disliked the thought of walking even for a short while with this aggressive young man, at least it gave her the opportunity to carry the poor little hedgehog off the road before it was killed.

She nodded and scrambled from the van before he could come round to help her out. But his long economic stride had taken him to the little pathetic brown ball even as she rounded the bonnet of the car, and he was picking it up gently.

'Come on, old chap,' he was saying in a very different tone of voice from the one in which he had used with her.

'This is hardly the place to camp. Let's put you out of harm's way, shall we?'

Very gently he held the small creature against his jacket and came towards her. For the first time she saw the trace of his smile reflected in his eyes. So this man was human, she thought, pleased and grateful that he had rescued the hedgehog from a cruel death.

Her smile transformed her face into a thing of beauty. Her brown eyes were eloquent with feeling.

'You know, for a moment I was sure you were going to run over the poor little thing,' she said.

'We country dwellers usually leave that kind of bestial act to you town people. No one need run over anything defenceless when a few moments of stopping the car and removing the creature to safety would suffice. A car is the most lethal weapon there is in the wrong hands.' He gestured to a gate at the side of the road opening on to a rough earth path up the hill. 'This way,' he added.

He was getting at her—nothing was so sure. When he had turned to close the gate after them she managed to still quivering emotions.

Her voice was quiet and low as they walked up the hill. 'Does Miss Moira Frazer feel the same way about me as you do?'

'I don't know.' He was staring straight ahead and from her vantage point well below his shoulder, his firm jaw took on a formidable jut. 'Were you necking when the accident happened?'

Vexation inside her at his behaviour now reached boiling point. 'How dare you sit in judgement on me when you know nothing of what really happened? I admit I was partly responsible for what happened, but not in the way you're insinuating.'

Her nails dug into the palms of her hands and she almost stumbled. What a horrible man he was! The only explanation for his rudeness must surely be that it had put him out in some way coming to meet her. Maybe a date with his girl-friend ... or his wife had quarrelled with him that morning and he was taking it out on herself. Whatever it was she would give him a wide berth in the future. Fore-warned was forearmed.

He said coolly, 'Is that why your boy-friend paid up so handsomely when he need not have done?'

Laraine bit her lip. Why should she tell him that it was at her own stubborn insistence on learning of the girl's in-juries ... never, perhaps, to walk again, to spend the rest of her life in a wheelchair ... that Harvey had settled a large sum on Moira Frazer.

'Since it doesn't concern you, I see no point in continuing this conversation,' she told him coldly.

In an attempt at composure she drew in long breaths of sweet fresh air. They had reached the summit of the hill, and they both stopped, Laraine to gaze around in admira-tion at the scene before her. Their only companions were the sheep and baby lambs dotting a panoramic view of open moorlands, and lush valleys with silver streamers of water gushing through them against a background of forests darkly rich with pine and birch.

Charles McGreyfarne gestured to the foothills where nestled a tiny village overlooked by a solid house rising slightly above it, on a small hill.

Laconically, he said, 'The Cheviots, and the gypsy pal-ace of Kirk Yetholm.'

Laraine looked down at the house. 'It isn't very big for a palace,' she said.

'Nevertheless it was one. It was the home of the gypsy kings of Scotland for centuries. Coronations were per-formed there and gypsies came from all over Britain for the celebrations. It has now been converted to a private house.'

Laraine laughed, a small tinkling sound that caught his attention, but she was oblivious of his gaze. She was imagining a land peopled by a fierce army of Borderers, big handsome horsemen, proud and independent, men who had inspired Walter Scott to immortalise them in his Waverley novels.

'How astonishing that there aren't hordes of sightseers

here,' she said almost to herself. 'It's all very inspiring, and very beautiful.'

'Blame that on the motorways, one on either side at the east and the west. I'm going down now to take our friend to the stream.'

Laraine followed his gaze down to a stream not far below beyond a sea of long rough grass. He did not suggest her going with him, but she did.

He went through the coarse grass easily and quickly in his riding breeches, but Laraine was not so lucky. Lagging far behind, she lost one of her court shoes and watched it roll down out of sight in the undergrowth. The last thing she wanted was to ask his help in looking for it, so she intensified her efforts to go down after it. Unfortunately her bare foot caught on a rock and she felt a sharp pain beneath it.

A sick sensation shot through her. Sweat oozed on her temples and she bit hard on her lip. Nevertheless, she continued down through the grass to grope around for her shoe.

'Having fun?' Charles McGreyfarne asked sardonically.

The face she lifted up to his was ashen. 'I've lost my shoe,' she said.

Roughly, he said, 'I didn't expect you to follow me. You aren't dressed for it.' His finger was hard beneath her chin. 'Are you hurt?'

She shook her head. The stabbing pain in her foot was now making her feel sick. 'I ... think my shoe is somewhere around.'

A ridiculous desire to weep on his shoulder possessed her, and she lowered her head to fight back the tears. But he made no attempt to look for the missing shoe. Instead he remained very quiet just looking down at her, while the imprint of where his finger had been still made itself felt on her chin.

'You have hurt yourself, haven't you?' he said at last. 'Lift your foot.'

'It's nothing ...' she began, and made no move.

'Then we'll see, shall we?' Kneeling beside her, he lifted

her foot to examine it underneath. 'Hmm, it appears to be a clean cut, and rather deep since it's bleeding quite a lot. I'm going to carry you down to the stream while I go to the horsebox for the first aid kit.'

He reached out to lift her bodily with consummate ease and made his way down to the stream, where he set her down gently on a small grassy bank beside the swiftly flowing water.

'Take off your stocking, and put your foot into the water. I'll be back,' he told her, and strode away.

Hurriedly, Laraine slipped off her stocking and did as she was told. The water was cool and after the first smarting sensation, the pain in her foot eased. Presently she lifted her foot rather gingerly to see a cut not more than an inch long but rather deep. It was still bleeding.

'I found your shoe. I left it in the horsebox.'

Laraine looked up to find him there beside her opening the first aid box in his hand.

'But I want my shoe to walk in,' she objected firmly.

He lowered himself down to take her injured foot on his knee as if he had not heard.

He said, 'I'm afraid this is going to sting for a moment.'

Laraine bit her lip and watched as he applied liquid from a small bottle on to a piece of cotton wool. It stung all right, but she stubbornly refused to let him see it hurt. In that moment he raised his eyes and she had the feeling of having touched a live wire when his eyes held her own captive.

'Sorry about that,' he said briefly. 'I'm going to put on a waterproof dressing.'

Laraine was quite pale, but her eyes were quite resolute and frank.

'Thank you. You're very kind,' she said.

'It was my fault,' he answered. 'I should have told you to stay where you were instead of following me.'

'I wouldn't have had it any other way since we saved the hedgehog.'

He applied the waterproof dressing in seconds very efficiently in the small of her instep, and said banteringly, 'Quite a small dainty foot, Cinderella. Shall we go?'

There was that in his voice that forbade further argument on her part. But she yielded against her will to the strength of his arms when he lifted her, and did not breathe properly again until he put her down gently in the horsebox and not in the cab. He had fixed a kind of bed of car blankets in which she could recline with her foot up.

'Sorry about putting you in here, but you'll be able to keep your leg up to stop the bleeding in your foot. I'll leave the door up so that you can see the scenery. How does it feel? Comfortable?'

'Much better, thanks,' she assured him. 'I have good healing skin. It will be better in no time.'

His eyes were on her shapely leg and small foot. 'I hardly think it will be healed when we reach McGreyfarne,' he said dryly.

Her brown eyes met his in dismay. 'McGreyfarne, did you say?'

'I did.' He was leaning negligently against the inner wall of the horsebox gazing down at her enigmatically.

'But I thought...' she began with instant anxiety.

'That you were going to Miss Frazer's home, Loch-doone?' He shrugged. 'Her father is away and she's staying at McGreyfarne.'

'Shall I be needed there?' she asked waveringly.

'You will,' he answered mildly. 'As a companion, not as a chaperone.'

Laraine blushed scarlet. 'I didn't mean it that way.'

'Why did you apply for the post anyway?' he probed placidly.

'Because I wanted to.'

'You mean you had a conscience?'

Laraine clenched her hands. What a hateful man! 'For-give me if I don't answer that one, won't you?' Her voice shook slightly despite her determination not to let him upset her. 'It may surprise you, I have sensibilities. I feel very deeply for other people.'

He regarded her in silence for a moment, then shook his head. 'I thought so. That's what I was afraid of.'

Tartly she said, 'I wouldn't say you were afraid of anything.'

'I'm not. But it doesn't alter the fact that you represent trouble.'

'For whom?'

'Shall we say Miss Frazer up to now?'

Laraine could have retorted that Moira Frazer had brought trouble on herself by her bad driving, but she remained silent. In her opinion the girl had more than paid for it. She closed her eyes and lay back on the cosy car rugs.

She must have fallen asleep, for the horsebox awoke her as it swerved on to a drive lined with trees. The trees continued for some distance before giving way eventually to well laid out grounds and flower beds. Presently they circled a fountain where a stone dryad held up the spray of water and pulled up outside the heavy oak-studded entrance door beneath an archway of fluted stone.

McGreyfarne was a pleasant two-storied building of solid stone. There was a turret on either side and deep eaves. Laraine, leaning out to look at it, put her hand on her missing shoe. She was putting it on when Charles McGreyfarne strolled around the back.

'Determined little cuss, aren't you?' he commented. 'I'd like the doctor to look at that foot.'

Laraine stood up and smoothed down her dress. The idea of her requiring a doctor filled her with dismay. He held up his arms and she placed her hands on his shoulders as he swung her to the ground.

She looked up at him earnestly as he released her. 'Please, no doctor. I'm sure the foot will be all right. You ... mentioned me causing trouble here, but that's something I'm determined not to do. I've had no pain since you put on the dressing except a feeling of soreness, which is only what one can expect.' He said nothing and she rambled on, 'I'm sure Miss Frazer sees enough of the doctor as it is without him coming to me. After all, she's to be my prime concern. I don't know why you're insisting when I have such...'

'Good healing skin,' he finished mockingly.

His eyes were critically intent upon her, his look enigmatic. Her face grew hot beneath his scrutiny as he drawled, 'I don't see why you should be averse to seeing the doctor. He's a perfectly nice man and happens to be a friend of the family. Also, while you're beneath our roof you are our responsibility.'

Her eyes moved downwards from his face. 'My foot will be fine,' she insisted, her voice very low.

'And if I insist?' he said quietly.

'I shall still refuse,' she asserted firmly, lifting her eyes to look him squarely in the face. 'You said just now that my presence here will bring trouble. I don't intend that this should be so. I'm sorry that you don't like me, but my job here has nothing to do with you.'

'No?' He was looking at her with steady eyes. 'I would like to think that.'

Something in his tone made her stiffen. There was unmistakable irony and something else that she could not define. A chill feathered over her skin like an east wind. He baffled her in the very carelessness of his attitude, which to say the least was oddly disconcerting. Maybe that was his intention—to make her feel out of place, not wanted. Well, his reception had put her on her mettle for similar ones!

His bow was slightly supercilious. 'McGreyfarne offers you its hospitality.' His hand was on her arm, and Laraine allowed him to lead her up the semicircular stone steps to the entrance without limping.

CHAPTER TWO

'AUNT MARGARET, this is Miss Laraine Winters. Miss Winters, my aunt, Miss Margaret McGreyfarne.'

Charles made the introduction smoothly. The young woman who came forward to greet them was as blonde as her nephew with the same crisply curling hair and narrow clear-cut features. She was much younger than Laraine had expected, not much older than Charles, with the same air of good breeding. Her blue tartan woollen skirt was topped by a cashmere sweater and she wore it with an air of simplicity and charm laced with dignity. Her smile, while reserved, was not lacking in warmth as she took Laraine's hand and cordially asked her to sit down in one of the spacious comfortable chairs by the huge fireplace.

As she sat down a red setter, who had been gazing up at her with soft brown eyes, rose from the hearth to thrust a cold wet nose on to her lap.

'Down, Mac!'

Charles spoke with an air of command as she fondled the dog's silky head and he obediently lay down on the hearth again at her feet.

'Did you have a good journey?' Margaret McGreyfarne asked, sitting down opposite to her to pour out tea from a silver pot. 'I hope you won't find it too dull after London.'

Laraine thought of the beautiful scenery, the lovely glens, and the enchanting village she had recently passed through, and said sincerely,

'I think it's beautiful country.' She accepted a cup of tea and refused sugar. 'I'm sure I could never be bored here. It's too lovely.'

'Are you easily bored, Miss Winters?'

Charles had accepted a cup of tea from his aunt and was

23

leaning back indolently against the side of the fireplace. Laraine described him to herself in that moment as tall, tanned and arrogant. She braced herself to meet his mocking gaze.

'I'm a working girl,' she said. 'As such I have no time to be bored.'

'Even so, McGreyfarne is no place for a gregarious person, as you'll discover.'

Laraine looked down into her cup, aware that though his words were spoken courteously they sounded in the nature of a snub.

'Since I came here to work I hardly expected to be entertained socially. Besides, it's the first time I've been to Scotland and the days will never be long enough for me to see everything.'

'You mustn't take any notice of Charles,' said Margaret McGreyfarne, passing a plate of biscuits for Laraine to help herself. 'I thought a biscuit would suffice until dinner this evening, unless you would prefer a sandwich. We dine in two hours' time at seven.'

Laraine smiled and was vexed to find her hand trembling a little as she helped herself to a biscuit. 'This is fine, thanks,' she said. 'I'm not all that hungry.'

It was true. What appetite she had was dulled by Charles' probing, almost analytic regard. She sipped her tea, constantly aware of him. On entering the room her first thought had been how spacious and lofty it was. Charles' long indolent figure narrowed the dimensions somewhat. There was no denying that he was in the right setting. She could never imagine him in a small suburban house or a cottage, but she wished that he was anywhere other than where he was at that moment.

She asked with an attempt at normality, 'Is Miss Frazer well?'

Margaret McGreyfarne finished a biscuit and washed it down with her tea. 'As well as she usually is these days, poor poppet. She's out at the moment.'

Her voice was filled with concern, a fact not missed by Laraine, who wondered if they were related.

There was a discreet knock on the door and a manservant appeared. He was of medium height, slim in stature, with thinning hair and a lined face.

He addressed Charles. 'I've taken the luggage upstairs and Morag says to tell the young lassie that her room be ready when she is.'

Instantly Laraine put down her cup and rose to her feet, anxious to seize the chance to go to her room. Charles straightened.

'This is Jock,' he said. 'He and his wife Morag are our most treasured possessions here at McGreyfarne. He'll take you to your room.'

Any kind of a room would have looked welcoming to Laraine as somewhere to escape to away from Charles McGreyfarne. It was, however, delightful, as delightful as the way leading up to it. The beautiful staircase swept gracefully to the upper regions with stained glass windows throwing stiffly spread fingers of coloured lights across the hall and on the high domed ceiling. The pine-panelled walls glowed softly and richly in the shadows and dazzling beams of light glanced off the crystal chandeliers.

Her room on the first floor was spaciously lofty with tall windows overlooking the front of the house and grounds. Morag, a small wiry woman very much like her husband, was waiting for her when she entered.

'I hope everything will be to your liking, miss,' she said courteously. 'I will leave you to do your own unpacking because then you will know where everything is. Let us know if there is anything you want.' At the door, she paused, looking neat and efficient in her black dress with a neat little tartan collar and cuffs. 'You will hear the gong go in the hall for dinner.'

Laraine unpacked her cases, deciding that she liked Margaret McGreyfarne, Jock and Morag, and Mac, the dog, but she did not definitely like Charles. Perhaps it was this last thought that influenced her choice of dress for the evening. It was cotton with a cool neckline and cap sleeves. In pale pink with a pattern of rainbow blended colours it was simplicity in itself, and her dark hair, like her warm skin, was very effective against it. The rainbow matching studs in her ears were her only adornment, leaving the slender line of her neck pure and uncluttered.

The result satisfied her—it was demure, and she did not want any snide remarks from Charles about her appearance. She went downstairs as the dinner gong went, not wanting to make a dramatic entrance when everyone else was there.

Charles was already there with a well-built young man in his thirties, but to her annoyance Laraine was only conscious of Charles McGreyfarne. He had changed into evening dress. Somehow it failed to subdue the aura of virile masculinity he seemed to convey. His body had the whipcord strength of active muscles, a body made fit by outdoor pursuits, making everything he wore seem correct. And those eagle eyes spoke of an active brain. Laraine felt his presence like the impact of a sudden shock, and decided to ignore it. He was looking at her with a quirk of those firmly cut lips, and Laraine was goaded into saying something rude when he spoke.

'Miss Winters,' he said carelessly, 'I want you to meet Rob McIndle. He looks after Lochdoone, Miss Frazer's home. Rob, Miss Laraine Winters. As you know, she is to become Moira's companion.'

Laraine smiled up at a man who reminded her of a husky gamekeeper. With his fresh complexion, well brushed brown hair and stalwart shoulders, she could imagine him patrolling the grounds of an estate with his gun under a stalwart arm. He looked to be in his early thirties, a rather serious type, but kind, she could tell that by his eyes. They twinkled.

'Delighted to meet you, Miss Winters,' he said warmly. 'Moira needs someone young and bright.'

'An aperitif, Miss Winters?' Charles had been in the act of pouring out drinks while standing talking to the other man when Laraine had entered the room. He now offered her a glass of sherry.

'No, thanks,' she said, without awkwardness. 'I don't drink.'

'That makes two of us.' Rob took her arm and leading her to a sofa, sat down beside her. His eyes held something more than interest. 'I can see Moira is going to be more than surprised to meet you. You have met?'

'I saw her at the hospital.' Laraine quivered. 'I was hoping that Miss Frazer had been as lucky as we had been in escaping serious injury.'

'But she wasn't.' Laraine looked up to see Charles towering above her with two glasses. 'Apple juice or tonic?' he said with a hint of satire.

'Apple juice, please,' she said.

'I'll take the tonic,' Rob grinned at him. 'Not that I need a tonic. It's surprising what the sight of a pretty girl can do.' He raised his glass. 'Here's to you, Miss Winters, for brightening up the landscape.'

'I didn't think it needed any brightening up,' she answered demurely. 'I find it fantastic.'

Charles had not moved. He was still standing there, his eyes sliding over the irrepressible Rob before resting on Laraine's pink cheeks and dancing eyes.

'Miss Winters happens to be engaged as Moira's companion, not yours, Rob,' he said curtly with an obliqueness meant to shatter her composure.

Laraine looked from one to the other, sensing a tenseness between the two men. But Rob appeared to be unrepentant.

'I don't need to be reminded since she'll be around in any case. I should like to take you out some time, Miss Winters. Do you ride?' he said.

A movement at the door prevented Laraine from answering. Turning her head, she saw the doorway contained a girl in a wheelchair which Margaret was pushing. A strange feeling of crisis sucked Laraine's throat dry. The room was suddenly very quiet, and looking at Moira, her compassions deepened. The last time she had seen the girl had been in a hospital bed, her hair tousled, her eyes closed spreading fans of thick lashes on her pale cheeks. Now she was seeing the girl as she really was except for the set of what should have been a pretty mouth, a mouth that was tight and weary now in a hopeless kind of way.

Her face in its aura of fair hair had the pale ethereal beauty of magnolia petals, her eyes, a pretty dark grey, were devoid of expression. As she came into the room she returned their greeting without really smiling. Her eyes were fixed steadily upon Laraine, who stood up as she approached.

Laraine never did remember the details of that meeting. But she did remember the way Moira sat at the table in her specially adapted wheelchair. Apart from her pallor there was nothing to suggest that she could not walk.

Her evening dress, halter-necked, showed off the sheen of lovely shoulders. Her slippers were silver, matching the bracelet on her arm, and stones glittered around her slender throat and at her ears like fire.

Laraine thought, she's utterly lovely with her lovely skin, and her fair hair so very effective against the midnight blue of her dress, a colour so flattering to blondes. I wish I knew what she really thinks about my part in the accident.

But Moira gave nothing away. She was like a beautiful statue, murmuring, 'How do you do,' in a cool detached little voice. Later, at the dining table, she had leaned across to say in an undertone, 'Perhaps you'll call to see me in my room before you go to bed.'

The meal was delicious—home-made soup, freshly caught salmon with a mouthwatering sauce, braised beef, then strawberries and cream. Laraine refused the cheeses and biscuits, deciding on a second cup of the delicious coffee. They drank the latter seated around the log fire with Margaret serving the coffee the second time round after Jock had left the room.

It seemed that even in summer the evenings were cool enough for a fire. Laraine looked around the beautiful gracious room with the firelight flickering on old furniture polished through the years with loving care. In the twilight Moira's necklace, the white of the men's collars and cuffs against their dark evening suits, the silver coffee set and the colourful décor of the room stood out clearly in a kind of sepia glow that Laraine would love to paint. So did the white smile of Charles, who was the urbane and amusing host.

Different topics of conversation were blended into the soft background music from a record player in which they all joined, Laraine included. It was all cosy and informal with no one treating her like a newcomer.

It was late when Charles wheeled Moira from the room and Laraine went with Margaret to see Rob leave in his estate car. It appeared that he had brought Moira back in it after an afternoon spent at Lochdoone during which she had gone through some business papers with him. As his car disappeared Margaret lifted her face to the sweet night air, and breathed in.

'I love the evenings best of all,' she said. 'There's a certain hush about it that's somehow so relaxing.'

Laraine felt her heart warming to the sweet-faced woman beside her. Strange that she had not married, she thought. She was very attractive and must surely have had suitors.

She said lightly, 'Then you must be a romantic. All romantics love the evenings. It has something to do with the moon.'

Margaret laughed. 'Well, I'm not waiting for it to come out tonight,' she replied, looking up at the floating clouds with the glow of the moon behind them. 'I always call in to see Moira before going to bed. You know where her rooms are? They're on the ground floor through the first door to the right of the staircase in the hall. Charles had the rooms prepared for her because of the wheelchair. Goodnight. Sleep well.'

Laraine lingered, knowing that she had to wait for Mar-

garet to leave Moira before going in to see her as requested.
Poor Moira, missing such a lovely evening, she mused,
gazing up at the sky as though to search for some miracle
that would heal her.

'Wishing on the moon?' said a deep voice. 'How's the
injured foot?'

Her heart missed a beat, then went racing on as Charles
loomed by her side. 'I ... I'd forgotten all about it,' she
stammered on breath regained.

'I hadn't. I've given Morag instructions to bathe and
dress it for you in the morning,' he drawled, pushing his
hands in his pockets and watching the sky. 'Here comes
your moon.'

The moon came slowly from behind the clouds to look
down on them blandly, and Laraine wished fervently that
her companion would go.

'It won't do, you know,' he said quietly. 'Or should I say
it won't work?'

Laraine braced herself. 'What won't work? Wishing on
the moon?'

'No. You coming here as Moira's companion.'

'Why not?'

'You're too young, for one thing. You and Moira are
about the same age, and you'll be a constant reminder of all
she's missing in the wheelchair.'

She looked up at him with a degree of anger and exasperation. 'Miss Frazer wants someone with her of her own
age. Besides, she might not always need the wheelchair.
The surgeon at the hospital could find nothing wrong with
her back. He reckoned that it was just a nerve somewhere
that could be put out of action temporarily.'

'And how do you know all this?'

'Because I went to see the surgeon myself when I heard
about Miss Frazer being discharged from the hospital.'

'So now you're hoping to be the one who'll work a
miracle to get Moira walking again?'

She said hotly, 'I didn't say that.'

'No, but you'll go all out to help her and end up all washed out yourself. Then we shall have two invalids on our hands.'

Laraine's voice was tart. 'I'm hoping that we shall be at Lochdoone by then. I'm sorry that it means me staying here until we leave, but I shall have to bear it.'

'Brave girl! Think how relieved you'll be when you finally leave.'

She lifted her chin. 'No more relieved than I am to leave you now,' she retorted. 'Believe me, it's a relief that's beyond words. Goodnight, Mr McGreyfarne.'

She went indoors pursued by a torrent of emotion which she knew was absurd. It was foolish to let the man upset her. By the time her room was reached she had regained a sense of calm, and the brief respite waiting for Margaret to make her way to her own room after visiting Moira gave her time to pull herself together. Fortunately Charles was nowhere in sight when she made her way downstairs again to Moira's room.

Moira lay in bed with her eyes closed. The pale silky hair was strewn across the pillow and there were shadows around her eyes. She looked vulnerable and pathetic.

Laraine bent over her. 'I hope I'm not disturbing you,' she said softly.

The pale lids fluttered open to reveal very attractive grey eyes with a circle of black around the iris. But they lacked warmth as she lowered a thick fringe of lashes.

She spoke without expression. 'I didn't engage you—it was my father's idea. He wanted me to have someone of my own age around. Sit down, won't you?'

Laraine sat down in a chair beside the bed, wanting to say the right thing. For the moment she could only feel a deep compassion for a girl cut down on the threshold of life. On the other hand, it had been a miracle that Moira had not been killed, coming out on her wrong side at a bend. Not that her life meant much to her in her present state. But Laraine thought of what the surgeon had said, that it was possible that she might walk again. Maybe it had been that ray of hope that had urged her on to see what she could do for the girl.

She said haltingly, 'I ... suppose you know I was in the other car when it hit you? I saw you later at the hospital. They let me go into your room for a moment before your father arrived.' She gave a pale smile. 'I felt so relieved to see that your face had escaped injury. You're so pretty.'

'And now I'm just a cabbage. A lot of good looks will do me now.'

Her voice was bitter and her mouth had thinned. Laraine bit her lip.

'But you won't always be like this. Lots of people have walked again after a temporary paralysis.'

'The physiotherapist said that at the hospital when I went for treatment. I only believed it for so long, but I don't now.'

Moira reached for a cigarette from a packet on the bed-side table and flicked a lighter. Laraine noticed the strained fingers, and her compassion increased.

'But surely the treatment at the hospital was something for you to do? It must have lessened the feeling of bore-dom,' she said.

Moira's laugh was bitter. 'You mean it was something to do besides smoking. Oh, I know I smoke too much, but it's supposed to calm my nerves.' She paused and looked at the glowing end of her cigarette. 'I knew you were one of the reasons I'm like this. Your boy-friend paid me quite a bit of conscience money.'

Laraine said in reasoning tones, 'It wasn't conscience money. I ... we had no idea how you were fixed for money and Harvey is a wealthy man. He'll never miss what he gave you.'

Moira blew a line of smoke into the air almost insolently. 'And he'll never know what it's like to be in a wheelchair. Are you going to marry him?'

'No. I never intended to. You have a beautiful part of the

country to recuperate in,' Laraine changed the subject. 'You're very lucky really to have all this clean fresh air and the natural beauty of your surroundings.'

Moira's voice was heavy with sarcasm. 'I'm very lucky, aren't I, to be able to see it all from a wheelchair. Why did you come? You knew you couldn't do much for me. There's sure to be some ulterior motive. Girls like you from the city aren't likely to come up here for an indefinite period unless there was something worthwhile.'

Laraine felt suddenly out of her depth. 'I wanted to help,' she replied quietly. 'When one receives a cruel blow from fate one should fight back. Make yourself believe that you will walk again and you will.'

'Just like that!' Moira snapped her fingers. 'I shall have to do, won't I, since I now have a rival?'

Laraine was annoyed but refused to be needled. 'I don't know what you mean by that,' she retorted, flushing.

Moira curled a lip. 'Don't tell me that you haven't noticed Charles as a man. It's pitiful the way the girls run after him at local gatherings. There's my father too. He's a very good-looking man for his age. I need hardly tell you that I hang on fiercely to what is mine.'

Laraine's breath caught queerly in her throat. 'I beg your pardon,' she said huskily. 'I don't understand.'

Moira tapped ash into an ashtray on the bedside table. 'Just don't begin to have any designs on either of them, that's all.'

'You mean ... you and Mr McGreyfarne ... are engaged?'

'Not officially, but it's understood that we shall marry.' The rest of the cigarette was suddenly stubbed into the ashtray. 'I know you'll regard me as a selfish pig to marry in my present condition, but Charles won't mind. He doesn't particularly want children, and the estate keeps him fully occupied.'

Laraine met the defiant look with compassion. 'Then don't you think that you have a good reason for walking again? I've had lessons in physiotherapy these last few months, so you see I did come with a goal in mind.'

Moira's face looked suddenly pinched. 'A real ministering angel, aren't you?' she jeered. 'Go away, you make my headache much worse.'

'Do you have bad heads?' Laraine was on her feet. 'Turn over on your front—I'll help you. Please let me.'

For a moment Moira held her shoulders rigid. Then she allowed herself to be turned over to rest on her stomach. There was silence in the room while Laraine massaged her neck and shoulders gently but firmly.

At last Moira admitted ungraciously, 'Thanks. That's much better.' She sighed. 'Leave me as I am. I'll be all right.'

'Sure you don't want me to shake your pillows?'

Laraine hovered and soon she saw the slim shoulders moving gently in sleep. Morag was there outside the door with a cup of hot milk on a tray.

'It's for the lassie to take with her sleeping pill,' she whispered.

'Miss Frazer is asleep. I'd leave it if I were you. I'll call at her room in an hour or so to see if she's still asleep. I can come down to the kitchen if she's awake to heat her some milk,' Laraine said.

Morag smiled. 'This will be the first time the lassie has gone to sleep without a sleeping pill. Not that I hold with them—I don't. Sleep is not beneficial if it doesn't come naturally. Thanks, I'll take it back only too glad to do so. Glad you've come. Goodnight, miss.'

In her room, Laraine thought of what Moira had said about her and Charles. She recalled the way he had looked at her earlier upon entering the dining room, the deep probing in his eyes. Later it had been Moira at whom he had looked, but that breathless state his regard had pushed her into could not be forgotten. She turned restlessly on her pillows, not understanding her own emotions. She could understand Moira wanting to keep the love of her father and also that of Charles—after all, they were her mainstays in a very lonely world. And it seemed that she had Margaret's love too. As for Charles, he was an enigma. So far she had only come up against his ruthless side. But he had great compassion. He had shown this clearly enough when he had rescued the poor little hedgehog, even to taking it to a safe place. Laraine pushed the thought away, knowing that while she did so it could never be discounted nor forgotten. Of one thing she was sure—and that was to help the unfortunate Moira with every means in her power, despite the churlishness of Charles McGreyfarne.

CHAPTER THREE

SHE awoke the following morning to the sun streaming in with a kiss of warmth. The bed had been beautifully comfortable and the thick walls had kept out all sounds. Stretching luxuriously, Laraine was tempted to leave her bed and run barefoot through the dew-wet grass until a sudden twinge in the instep of her injured foot reminded her that Morag was coming in to dress it. It was so unnecessary to give the poor woman an extra chore, but Charles seemed determined to prove his own statement that she would bring trouble. Bother Charles, she thought, and padded to her window to watch the sun over the glen and breathe in what seemed to be a tang of sea air. How beautiful it was, and not a bit alien to a stranger like herself.

The bath water was lovely and hot, stinging her injured foot, then soothing it. Fortunately there was a box of waterproof adhesive dressings in the bathroom cabinet and she applied a fresh one to the wound. Then clad in a sweater and slacks, she made her way to Moira's room.

Moira was lying fast asleep in the same position that Laraine had left her in the previous evening after massaging her neck and shoulders. Keeping her word to Morag, she had slipped into her room several times during the night and had fallen asleep herself long after dawn.

Morag was waiting for her at the door of her room.

'Moira is still asleep,' Laraine told her, at the same time looking at the tray containing things for bathing and dressing her foot. 'I've dressed my foot, Morag—I used a dressing from the bathroom cabinet.'

Morag looked worried. 'Are you sure it's all right? Mr Charles gave instructions for me to bathe it in salt water, dress it and report to him.'

Laraine smiled. 'Mr McGreyfarne is making too much fuss over nothing,' she said reassuringly. 'I'll see him.'

Morag nodded, not altogether happy. 'Breakfast is in the dining room.'

As Laraine made her way across the hall Charles came in with Mac at his heels. Once again she felt the impact of his magnetism as he strode in with the loose-limbed grace of a man healthy in wind and limb. His skin had that ruddy bronze tan bestowed by sun, wind, and rain, bringing with him the tang of fresh morning air. He was dressed in riding breeches, and a loose sweater. His thick blond hair was wind blown and he studied her with his usual maddening calm.

'Good morning, Miss Winters,' he said, adding as Mac ran to her, 'Down, Mac. To the kitchen pronto!'

He clicked his fingers and the dog obeyed. Then he slanted a gaze down at Laraine, who was smiling as they entered the dining room.

'Something amuse you?' he asked.

'Yes, but I hadn't better tell you what it is.'

'Why not? Might as well say it as think it.'

He drew out a chair at the table and Laraine allowed him to seat her before speaking.

Picking up her table napkin, she said, 'I was imagining you clicking your fingers in that same arrogant fashion to a wife. Are the Scots lassies docile?'

Her smile was demure, and for a moment a gleam came into his eyes. It was gone before she could define it. His smile was sharp, matching the crisp and cynical tone of his voice.

'I haven't noticed one way or the other. We Scots might descend from a savage race of Borderers, but we do now manage to live in a civilised manner. The traditions of the past are still dormant within us and we're a fiercely independent and proud race.' The firm mouth lifted a little at the corners. 'However, we respect and love our women, our land and our heritage.'

Laraine looked up to meet his intent gaze and her sense of humour got the better of her. She laughed, a pleasing quiet sound, at which he raised a brow.

'I'm sorry,' she said. 'I shouldn't have said what I did, but I've never met anyone like you before. Tell me about McGreyfarne and if we're near the sea. I ask because I distinctly felt it in the air this morning as I stood at my window.'

He poured out coffee and passed her a cup, saying lazily, 'We're only half a mile from the beach. Do you swim?'

'Yes. But that wasn't the reason I was interested. It occurred to me that Miss Frazer and I might have picnics on the beach. Is her home, Lochdoone, far away?'

'The other side of the village. Incidentally, Rob McIndle isn't married, but that doesn't mean that he hasn't an eye for the girls. Managing Lochdoone is the first job he has had after frittering away his part of the family fortunes. The amazing thing is that he really is quite likeable and a good sport. But all he has at the moment is a small annuity from a doting mother and his salary from Lochdoone, which isn't much.'

Jock came in at that moment with hot covered dishes containing a substantial breakfast for far more than two people. Laraine gazed helplessly at an array of bacon, eggs, sausages and tomatoes, and freshly baked oatcakes. Taking a little of each on to her hot plate, she was thankful to see Margaret arrive and take her seat at the table.

The meal progressed, with Margaret asking her questions about what she had done prior to taking her present post, and her former life in general. No mention was made of the reason she was here at McGreyfarne or the accident. Up to now Laraine had not been very clear what kind of role Margaret played at McGreyfarne. It was obvious that she acted as hostess for Charles, but she must have some kind of hobby, surely?

As if on cue, Magaret asked politely, 'Have you any hobbies, Miss Winters?'

'I paint in my spare time,' she confessed. 'Nothing spectacular. I thought I might get Miss Frazer interested. After all, it's something she can do without any strain or discomfort. I happened to have a very talented artist neighbour in the flats where I lived. He helped me quite a lot.'

'Really? Have you any of your pictures with you?' Margaret asked.

'No.' It was on the tip of her tongue to say that she had sold several of her paintings since taking up the hobby two years ago, but something in Charles' mocking gaze stopped her.

'It seems that Miss Winters has come fully prepared to clear all obstacles where Moira is concerned,' he remarked dryly. 'By the way, this is the day the ambulance collects her for the physiotherapy, isn't it?'

Margaret looked uncomfortable. 'She doesn't go any more. I suppose the ambulance will come as usual to see if she's changed her mind. She sent it back last week.'

'Did she now?' Charles looked thoughtful. 'I'll have a word with her.'

'Poor Moira,' said Margaret when her nephew had left the room. 'If anyone can persuade her to go, Charles can. More coffee?'

Laraine shook her head and watched her companion pour out the last of the coffee from the silver pot, then she said, 'I would like to go with Miss Frazer to the hospital if I may. She's sure to feel better with company.'

Margaret spooned brown sugar in her cup. 'Charles takes her to the door and lifts her out into the wheelchair provided to take her into the hospital. The ambulance brings her back. Last week Charles was away, so she refused to go.'

Laraine folded her table napkin and said, 'Mr McGreyfarne is very forceful.' She almost added, and arrogant.

Margaret smiled. 'Yes, he is. He's good for Moira because her father spoils her dreadfully. George Frazer allows his heart to rule his head where his daughter is concerned.

Moira was staying in London when the accident happened. She had got in with a rather Bohemian crowd and had borrowed the Mini in which she was injured from a friend. Since her mother died years ago her father hasn't denied her a thing.' Margaret sipped her coffee, her eyes clouded in memories. 'The trouble is both father and daughter are so likeable. There's nothing I wouldn't do for them.'

'Pity he didn't marry again,' Laraine commented, placing the folded napkin on the table.

'I'm afraid Moira has always been too possessive to allow him to.'

Probing beneath this information, Laraine pieced together the jigsaw of Lochdoone House. Moira was the spoiled child clinging on to the people around her regardless of anyone's happiness but her own. Now fate had played into her greedy little hands by placing her in the position to demand and go on demanding her own selfish needs and wants. If Laraine was not mistaken Margaret's feelings for George Frazer had gone beyond that of a friend, and she wondered if his feelings towards her were the same, and if this was so she admired Margaret greatly for bearing no malice against Moira.

'I see what you mean,' she said dryly. 'All the same, it's a great pity for one person to be allowed to spoil other people's lives.'

Margaret drank the rest of her coffee and put down her cup. 'I wouldn't say that Moira has spoiled anyone's life. She has brought much joy to her father, and like I said, she's very likeable. No, it's just one of those things.'. She lifted her head at the sound of a car starting outside the house. 'That will be Charles taking Moira to the hospital for treatment. What about coming with me into the garden to cut flowers for the house?'

They were returning to the house when Charles arrived in his car. Both women carried long flower baskets filled with blooms. His eyes slid over them both to narrow slightly at Laraine's sweet face above the flowers.

'Pity I haven't a camera,' he said. 'Moira is now at the hospital where she'll be for the next two hours. I see you're busy.'

They all walked slowly to the house. At the door Margaret said,

'What about taking Laraine around the estate? She hasn't seen any of it yet.'

Charles stood still, thrusting his hands into his pockets. 'I've too much to do. I'm expecting a man to call about the drainage.'

'If you mean Eddie Flowers, he won't be calling until after lunch. He's gone to a wedding this morning,' Margaret said matter-of-factly. 'There's nothing to stop you taking Laraine to the village. I'm sure she will enjoy it, and you can be back for lunch.'

Laraine watched her walk into the house with some alarm. An outing with the dour Charles was something she would prefer to avoid. Furthermore, the last thing she wanted was to be shown around the countryside from a sense of duty.

She said firmly, looking no higher than his broad chest, 'You don't have to put yourself out on my account. I prefer to wait until Miss Frazer returns. After all, I'm not a guest here. Your aunt means well, but I prefer to do my sightseeing alone. And now if you'll excuse me . . .'

She stalked past him with her chin in the air and to her own annoyance tripped up the first semi-circular step leading up to the doorway of the house. Instantly his hand shot out and gripped her arm to save her from pitching forward.

'Now now,' he chided in his maddeningly cool voice. 'Pride goes before a fall. Of course I'll take you to the village. As a matter of fact I have to call upon the vicar.' His eyes slid over her shapeliness in the slacks and sweater. 'I'll see you in the car in ten minutes.'

Laraine was unaware of the startled look in her clear eyes as he stood still gripping her arm. But she was aware of a curious disturbance around her heart, aware also of his male attractiveness, his tanned face, lean, finely chiselled jaw above the polo neck of his sweater, and his masterful arrogance. He was too cool, too self-possessed, and too dangerous.

He dropped his hand from her arm and spoke with some amusement. 'I know I'm not the ideal companion in your eyes, but you're quite safe with me, and I do promise to make the outing interesting.'

Laraine went indoors beyond words. Her arm was still tingling where he had gripped and her whole body had responded to his touch. His gaze had been both tantalising and mocking ... as though he was aware of her uneasiness in his presence. Pity she had to put up with him. The thing was to play it cool. Ten minutes later she was at the door going out to the car. He was already there, smoking a cigarette which he put out by grinding it into the gravel with his heel. Then he was opening the front door of the car for her to slide in. The gravel crunched as he went to sit in beside her behind the wheel and Laraine parried a small thrust of worry when he set the car moving.

'How is the foot?' he asked. 'Morag tells me you dressed it yourself. Was that wise? It was deep enough to require a dousing of salt water to be on the safe side. I hope it was starting to heal.'

'It was. I soaked it well during my bath and the waterproof adhesive dressing is antiseptic. Anyway, I can't feel any ill effects yet.'

He said darkly, 'Let's hope you don't. Now where do you want to go? Around the estate or to the village?'

'I thought you wanted to see the vicar?' she said.

'I do,' he replied sardonically. 'And it's about something which you will no doubt be interested in.'

'Is it?' Laraine answered warily refusing to be drawn into any conflict because he was sure to win. Those knowledgeable eyes of his gave her the feeling of being naïve and inexperienced. 'Why me?'

'Because you're an incurable romantic. We're to discuss

the problem of the gypsies in these parts. They need some-where to put up for a while, and the vicar wants my views on the subject.'

'You mean he wants you to let them have a field? Why not? You probably came from gypsy folk yourself right back in the past. My father taught us to live and let live.'

'And now you also love and let love.'

'That isn't funny,' Laraine retorted hotly. 'If you're implying that I was Harvey Strang's mistress you couldn't be more wrong. I admit lots of people do appear to be living together if you believe the press, but there are many more who are decent and clean-living, and I happen to be one of them.'

'Tut, tut,' he chided. 'No need to be angry, I was only teasing.' He threw a quick glance at her flushed cheeks and bright angry eyes and his mouth lifted at the corners. 'You know, you're quite something when you're angry.'

'You wanted me to be, didn't you?' she accused him. 'It must be that gypsy streak in you coming out. I bet you've had your moments.'

'So I have. Never mind, I'm sure you'll smile when I tell you that I'm giving the gypsies a field. There's plenty of fish to be caught in the fast-flowing little burns that abound, and no doubt they'll be industrious enough to use their fingers in weaving and whittling wooden things to sell in the little market towns. The village is quite interesting.'

Laraine loved the village square surrounded by buildings roofed in by sandy millstone glowing in the sun. There was evidence that centuries ago it was just a monastery and most of it remained in the small abbey, the inn and the tiny post office. The manse was close by and near to the little church, but the vicar had been called out to one of the outlying cottages. Charles took her to the little church, showed her around quaint buildings and explained their history. Then he waited in the car while she bought stamps at the post office.

They were on their way back to McGreyfarne when he

told her about the ghost that haunted the village. Years ago when the village was still a monastery Scottish raiders ruled the land. One dark night the monks heard the jingle of harness as a raiding party rode by, and they held their breath, praying for deliverance. Fortunately the monastery was well hidden by trees, so the raiders continued on their way unaware of its existence. It was then that a young monk, so overjoyed that they had been spared, rang out a peal of bells in thanksgiving for their deliverance. He had hardly released the bell rope when the raiders turned back on hearing the bells and promptly attacked them all.

Listening to Charles' deep voice, Laraine imagined one of his ancestors leading the raiding party. To her mind he came from stock that was too virile, too much male to lead a gentle life in a village. Yet he had been gentle with the hedgehog, behaving as if he hated killing for killing's sake. She fell to thinking what kind of a husband he would make—an exciting one, a gentle one? Angry with herself for allowing her thoughts to run away with her, Laraine was aware of him finishing his story.

'Now that poor misguided monk comes back to haunt the place in his torment, wringing his hands and wailing his distress.'

Laraine said on a quiver, 'Has anyone seen him?'

'Some people swear to having seen him, others to hearing him.'

They sped along roads past trout streams and between hedgerows of primroses and soft pink blossom hugging fresh green meadows open to a flawless blue sky. On a sudden rise Laraine looked towards the hills to see a line of horsemen with a standard-bearer leading.

Charles explained, 'One of the many teams taking part in what we call in this part of the world Common Riding. Common Ridings go on all over the country at this time of the year to commemorate ancient famous battles.'

He swung the big car off the country road on to the highway and put on speed. Laraine sat up as scattered farms gave way to a kind of suburb of small houses.

'I don't remember coming this way,' she said.

Charles made no answer but swung the car along an avenue of trees to his right to eventually stop before the entrance to the hospital.

She looked at him with startled surprise. 'Why didn't you say we were going to pick Moira up?'

He slid from the car and came round to open her door. 'Like to come in with me?' he asked, tongue in cheek.

As they entered Laraine could see Moira waiting in a wheelchair near to the reception desk. She was leafing through a magazine. A nursing Sister approached and Charles gave her a charming smile.

'Is this the young lady you spoke about, Mr McGreyfarne?' she asked, with a curious look at Laraine.

'It is.' He turned to look down into Laraine's astonished face and said coolly. 'We'll wait for you in the car while Sister examines your foot.'

Laraine had calmed down somewhat when her foot had been examined and dressed by the nurse. But she still smarted at Charles' high-handedness. How dared he? It was clear that he had made the appointment when he brought Moira earlier on. His manly charms had been sufficient to ensure that she would have immediate attention on arrival, and so she had. The nurse, however, had been satisfied that the cut, though deep, was going on nicely. There was no reason why it should not be healed quite soon if Laraine carried on with bathing it and keeping the dressing fresh. But she did agree with Mr McGreyfarne that one could not be too careful of infection where injuries were concerned. She was pleased that his mind would now be settled over the matter.

But the look she gave Laraine was a little puzzled. It must be common knowledge at the hospital that the tall, handsome Charles McGreyfarne had something in common with their outpatient Moira Frazer, yet here he was very concerned and showing it by another young woman's injury.

It was on the tip of Laraine's tongue to tell the nurse that there was no romance where she and Charles were concerned, but it was none of her business to disclose the reason why she was at McGreyfarne.

Moira was already seated in the front seat of the car beside Charles when Laraine left the hospital. She looked a little sulky, and Laraine did not blame her. The girl had had enough of the hospital without waiting around for herself to receive treatment.

'All right?' Charles asked, opening the door to the back seat for her. 'I did originally plan to bring you here when I picked up Moira.'

She nodded and replied politely without looking at him, and Moira turned in her seat towards her.

'You didn't mention the injured foot last evening,' she said. 'I hope it's better.'

Her voice was cool and detached. There was no concern, only a hidden irritation at not being the centre of attraction herself. It was something new for her to have her nose pushed out of joint, Laraine thought without rancour. Her sympathy was all with the girl who now had her back to the wall in her fight to keep those she loved around her. Consequently she replied that the accident had not been that important and that it was healing nicely.

On the short drive back to McGreyfarne she tried to reassure herself that all would be well between her and Moira when they once became really acquainted. After what now would be a late lunch, she might use suitable persuasion to get her patient to try her hand at painting.

But on arrival at McGreyfarne Moira asked Charles to carry her up to her room to have her lunch there. Margaret came to meet them at the door and Charles paused long enough with Moira in his arms to state that he would have lunch in his study in order to catch up on his work.

So Laraine and Margaret had lunch together. They were lingering over coffee on the terrace in the sun when Margaret said, 'I don't know what's got into Charles these last few days. He isn't a bit like his usual self. I can only put it down to having Moira under his roof. I wish they would get married and put an end to all the uncertainty.'

Laraine recalled the odd feeling inside her at the sight of Moira in Charles' arms and wondered what had got into her.

She said, 'I'm awfully sorry that things had turned out like they have. You see, I feel partly to blame for the accident.'

Margaret looked at her in surprise. 'But you weren't driving, so how could you be?'

'I upset Harvey as he was driving. You see, he'd proposed to me and I refused him. I ought to have put off my answer for a more opportune moment.'

'I don't agree. There's nothing more cruel than having false hopes. Better to wipe the slate clean.'

Margaret was so adamant that Laraine stared at her in surprise.

'So you don't blame me for what happened?'

Margaret laughed. 'Good gracious, no. I must confess that I was a little surprised when you applied for the job of companion to Moira, though. But I'm glad you did. You'll be good for her. I made the remark just now about Charles because I didn't want you to be upset by him. He's acting completely out of character, and I can only assume that he's finding the continued presence of the woman he loves too much to take.'

Laraine found Moira in her room sitting by the window in her wheelchair. She wondered how much she had eaten of her lunch and was sure that it was not much. Beyond turning her head to bid Laraine to enter, Moira said nothing.

'What about going out in the grounds?' Laraine suggested.

'What for?' Moira asked ungraciously.

Laraine shrugged helplessly with the feeling that she was making the wrong approach.

'For one thing,' she said firmly, 'the fresh air will do you good, and you might like to paint the scenery. It's so beautiful.'

'I can't paint.'

'You don't know what you can do until you try. I'll take you out, then fetch my painting things. You'll find it quite easy to hold a sketching block on your knees. At least you might get a laugh out of it.'

Moira looked her sullenly in the eye. 'I'd like to know what I've got to laugh about.'

But Laraine was already behind the wheelchair, pushing it across the room and through the open French windows to the garden.

Looking down at the fair head, she said, 'The people who are worth while are those who can laugh in the face of adversity. Since you're determined to stay in a wheelchair for the rest of your life it's up to you.'

'Who says I want to stay in a wheelchair? I haven't.'

Laraine looked around for a sheltered spot and spied a sunny corner at the end of the terrace.

'Your behaviour speaks for itself,' she answered, manoeuvring the wheelchair so that it faced a panoramic view of the hills. 'There, did you ever see such a view? I'll fetch my paints. Don't go away.'

Moira scowled at her attempt at gaiety.

When she returned Moira was staring unseeingly ahead, and did not even acknowledge her presence. She completely ignored the sketching block which Laraine offered. Full of compassion, she felt an odd quiver in her throat as she saw the tears glistening on Moira's thick lashes. Then putting down the sketching block, she began to set up the portable easel and canvas topped stool. They were lightweight and clipped on easily to the top of her suitcase, and Laraine blessed the thought that had urged her to bring them.

'Oh no, that can't be me! I look awful!' Moira wailed. She stared aghast at the sketch Laraine had drawn, her expression horrified. 'Why, my mouth is a tight straight line and all drawn in and there are frown lines on my face. I look really old.' She looked distressed. 'I don't really look like this, surely?' she pleaded.

Laraine said, 'That was how you were looking when I sketched you. That was your expression. There's a saying something about our eyes being what we are and our mouth what life has made us.' She took the portrait away and put a fresh block in its place in Moira's hands. 'There, you can have your revenge. Sketch me while I draw another one of you—and you'd better alter your expression!'

She sat down for several moments until Moira began to draw, gradually becoming engrossed in what she was doing. Then Laraine began to draw too. There had been one bad moment when she had thought that Moira was going to refuse, but the sketch of her had done the trick. Well, at least she had shaken her into some action, and out of that appalling lethargy.

As Moira became absorbed in her sketching the petulant droop of her mouth disappeared and her lips became sweetly curving. Her grey eyes softened and her whole expression altered. Taking advantage of this, Laraine worked swiftly and finished the portrait with a flourish, feeling well pleased with the result. Then she sat patiently waiting for Moira to finish her sketch.

At last Moira sat back and they exchanged sketches. Laraine accepted hers and waited for Moira's reaction. Slowly the warm colour mounted in her pale cheeks. Her grey eyes widened in surprise and wonder. Twice she opened her mouth to speak, but no words came.

At length, she said in a kind of awe, 'Is this really me? I look so different. I can't believe it . . . no lines on my face. It's lovely!' Her eyes were suddenly over-bright. 'I've allowed myself to become bitter, haven't I? I see that now. I would like to keep these sketches as a reminder. May I?'

Laraine nodded, full of compassion. 'Do so by all means. It's only natural for you to feel bitter, but it doesn't solve a thing, does it?'

Moira sighed heavily, 'No. I wish I could draw like that.'

Laraine smiled with a determination to keep it light. 'Be thankful that you can look so beautiful. Anyone can learn to draw and paint,' she said brightly. 'And now let's take a look at my portrait. Good heavens!' One look at Moira's sketch of herself was enough to send her into soft peals of laughter. At last, wiping the tears of mirth from her eyes, she gurgled helplessly, 'While I don't object to having one eye higher than the other I do object to that nose!'

Moira was contrite. 'Sorry. I told you I couldn't draw.'

For a moment the stubborn look was back on her face, but meeting Laraine's dancing eyes, she suddenly relaxed and began to giggle. Soon they were both laughing.

'Well, well, Moira laughing and enjoying it. Won't you let me in on the joke?'

Charles was striding towards them from the French window of the terrace with a charming smile. Then he was grinning down at Moira with such undoubted pleasure that Laraine felt a twinge near her heart. She quivered inside, wondering if the twinge was one of jealousy. It couldn't be, since she was not given to jealousy. At least not until now.

Moira shone up at him as he bent down to look at the sketch in her hands. He raised a brow and took it from her to study it intently.

'Hmm, not bad. Not bad at all. Did you do it?' he asked.

'Good heavens, no. Laraine did. She's going to give me painting lessons.'

Charles was still smiling down at her before turning indolently to look at Laraine. The curve of his mouth went slightly and so did the smile in his eyes.

'Quite professional, Miss Winters.'

'Thanks,' Laraine replied flippantly. 'Glad you think so. The scenery around here is so fabulous that I wonder there are not more artists around.'

'Maybe the men in these parts prefer more manly pursuits. Speaking from a male point of view, of course. Ever seen any Highland Games, Miss Winters?'

He returned the sketch to Moira and gave Laraine his full attention, shoving his hands into his pockets. Laraine felt the colour heating her face.

'No,' she admitted, gazing at him levelly. 'But I would say that tossing a caber is only another kind of skill than that of applying a paint brush to canvas. My artist neighbour is as male as you are.'

Unconsciously her nerves had tightened, and her eyes held a resentful gleam. However, she held herself rigid and controlled.

'The man certainly left an impression on you. Ever considered taking art up professionally?' he queried unperturbed.

'No. It doesn't appeal to me in that way. I just do it as a hobby. I'm glad I've taken it up, though, because I can help others to enjoy it too. You want to try it, Mr McGreyfarne. I'm sure you'll find it most relaxing. It might even take the edge off that cynicism that you're so fond of airing.'

'Wow!' put in Moira. 'Have you two quarrelled, or are you leading up to it?' There was a pleased look in her eye as she gazed from one to the other. 'I suggest that while we're here, Charles, we all use our first names. That should make your sparring a little more realistic, but don't come to blows, will you?' she ended sweetly.

Just then Morag appeared wheeling a trolley containing tea, and to tell Charles that he was wanted on the telephone. Laraine watched him go with a sense of relief, and immediately forgot him in the pleasure of seeing Moira look as if she was going to enjoy her tea. In her opinion the girl did not eat enough and smoked far too much. She desperately needed some kind of a hobby to occupy her time and help her to forget her immobility. Laraine hoped fervently that she could keep alive her interest in drawing and painting.

CHAPTER FOUR

ROB McINDLE came to dinner again that evening. He had been asked to stay after bringing some mail for Moira from Lochdoone. The vicar was there too, a slightly built little man with thin features and a warm friendly look. Laraine felt at ease with him and was glad to have him for a dinner partner. Rob was seated on her other side next to Margaret, then Charles with Moira.

As it happened Laraine quite enjoyed the meal, with the vicar telling her amusing incidents of his life at the manse. He made her laugh on several occasions, a sweet tinkling sound that was soft and musical on the ear. Her face had been radiant with mirth, her nose wrinkled in an endearing grimace, and her eyes sparkled with merriment. Charles glanced at her keenly but made no comment. Laraine had tried to ignore his presence, but it had been hopeless from the start. The trouble was that she was discovering qualities about him that contributed to his devastating charm. He had a sense of humour, and his wit, though razor-sharp at times, was wholly entertaining. And he had the kind of smile to tie any feminine heart into knots.

He would enter into any argument lazily and emerge the victor, although he never lost his temper or set himself out to be the victor. The disturbing quality of his personality lay in the way he had of holding himself aloof from a too familiar contact. Laraine looked at him with senses sharpened by the antagonism he had shown towards her, and felt his charm as something tangible. There was nothing to it, she told herself fiercely; it was only the fascination that any good-looking bachelor holds for any unattached woman. During her delightful conversation with the vicar she had also studied Moira, wanting with all her heart for the girl to come to life and behave normally again.

But Moira ate little, talked even less, and when Charles was not talking to her lapsed into an unhappy world of her own. Laraine understood that she was finding it harder to adjust than most girls to her new way of life. After all, she had always had her own way in life, always done exactly what she wished, and in all probability still cherished that same philosophy. But she was not a child any more, and if the accident had taken away her precious freedom, it had also helped her to mature.

In a way Laraine's compassion was tinged with impatience since Moira was showing no spirit. Instead of meekly accepting her lot she should be fighting against it for all she was worth. But Moira had never had to fight for anything. She had only to crook a dainty finger and whatever she wanted was there.

After dinner Charles took the vicar to his study for the discussion they should have had that morning, and Margaret suggested a game of Scrabble.

They played, Margaret, Moira, Rob and herself, until Charles and the vicar joined them. Then Jock come in with refreshment and a drink to finish off the evening. It was late when Laraine went to Moira's room at her request again before going to bed. Moira was sitting up in bed looking very pale but appealing. The dark shadows beneath her eyes enhanced her pallor and lent a delicacy to her features that a man would find pleasing because it appealed to his protective instincts. But Laraine sensed that the dark shadows beneath her eyes owed their presence to a bad headache.

'Relax,' she said gently as Moira lay on her front for her to massage her back and shoulders. Then to put her at her ease, she added, 'How did the treatment at the hospital go this time?'

Moira's voice was deadpan. 'Much the same. Did you know that Daddy had gone to Rome to see an orthopaedic man who specialises in cases like mine?'

'No, I didn't, but I'm very glad to hear it. They do such wonderful things these days. Does that mean you going to Rome for treatment?'

'If I go. I'm sick and tired of being prodded and examined without any result,' Moira complained bitterly.

Laraine moved slender fingers over the smooth shoulders and felt the tension in them lessen.

'But surely that's how results are obtained, by examinations? You'll soon forget all this when you're up and walking again,' she said cheerfully.

'I wish I could believe that,' Moira retorted, and said no more. She was asleep before Laraine left her room.

Before going to her own room she went to find Morag to tell her that once again her charge had gone to sleep without the aid of a sleeping pill. Then she made her way from the kitchen quarters into the grounds for a short walk before going to bed. A pale moon was shining already, although it was not dark. Laraine was beginning to love the quietness of sweet sounds, the wholesome scent of the pines mingling with the sea air, and above all, a land where so much about the past remained beautifully undisturbed.

There was an infectious tranquillity about the place that had stood still in time resisting all pressures, a sense of a stable security sadly missing in the hurly-burly of a modern everyday life. There was a sense of romance also, enhanced by the delicate perfume of the roses that abounded all around her. In the distance the hills lay sleeping in their misty night attire of mauves and greens, while the pines stood like dark proud sentinels watching over them.

'Don't you know better than to come out into the cool air without a wrap at this late hour?'

Before Laraine could turn around something warm and heavy was dropped across her shoulders, and she swung around to see Charles towering above her in shirt sleeves, having given her his dinner jacket.

For what seemed an age they stood looking at each other without speech. In the purple twilight his blond hair took on a luminous glow and his eyes gleamed angrily. Laraine looked no higher than his shirt front. She could not look up into his eyes other than with a swift glance because than she would have to look at that clean-cut firm mouth that moved her so strangely. In the blur of white shirt and dark slacks he looked even more male and to Laraine, his masculinity was overpowering. She grew tense as she felt the warmth of his jacket seeping into her. She had never felt so strange in her life.

But she spoke normally. 'You didn't have to take your jacket off even if I have come out without a wrap. I only intended to take a short walk. Please take it back.'

Her hand rose to slip the jacket from her shoulders, and in the next instant his hands were covering hers in no uncertain manner.

'You will leave it on until we return indoors,' he commanded curtly. 'What's the matter, don't you like the idea of a man's jacket around you?' He sounded suddenly sardonic. 'What were you running away from, a man's arms?'

She quivered. The grip of his hands was sending little fires through her whole being, bringing her alive from top to toe. To her everlasting shame she wanted him to take her in his arms and feel the pressure of his firm mouth upon her own. Wildly she wondered if she had better see a psychiatrist. Only an idiot would be drawn to a man who obviously had no time for her. Why, the man was detestable!

With a dignity that sat well on her slender shoulders, Laraine freed her hands from his clasp and said, with a valiant attempt at normality,

'I'm not running away from any one person. You can't believe, can you, that it's possible for someone to want to do something worthwhile, and without anything in it to their own advantage.'

'You don't have to remind me why you've come,' he said dryly. 'You make it clear enough by your actions.' He moved his tongue in his cheek and eyed her sardonically. 'Let's hope that in helping Moira you don't cause her any further distress.'

Laraine clenched her hands. He was hopeless! He could

not or would not see that Moira was her first and last concern.

'You'd better explain that last remark,' she told him coldly. 'How on earth can I possibly cause her further distress when I'm only here to do everything possible for her?'

He smiled satirically. 'When a person is confined to a wheelchair their world narrows down to a few people. Moira's friends include her father, Rob and myself—all males. I need hardly point out that a very attractive girl like you constitutes a threat to her small entourage.'

Dismay was uppermost in her voice. 'You don't seriously think that I came here with a husband in mind?' She swallowed on a dry throat, and tried to stem the feeling of anger at his unjust insinuations as she felt his gaze on her face. 'I've never heard anything so ridiculous in my life! What a horrible mind you must have!'

He gave a half smile. 'Not exactly. Already you have Rob McIndle hanging around.'

Hotly she looked up into his eyes, and retorted furiously, 'That's a lie!'

'Is it? Then why isn't Rob sending Moira's mail over as he has always done?'

'You mean that he brought it over today as an excuse to see me? Well, at least he's a gentleman, and that's more than I can say of you. And he is very likeable too, which you are not.'

'So you're taken with him already?' he said, patently sure.

'I like him. Why shouldn't I?' She looked him straight in the eye. 'He's fun to be with and he doesn't make sly innuendoes.'

'Rob is like that,' he replied unperturbed. 'He's run through a fortune since he was twenty-one, which is pretty good going since he hasn't yet reached thirty ... He's as irresponsible as they come.'

'We can't all be perfect. And if he's such a bad hat surely Moira is better off without him around?' Laraine paused and again wrinkled her brow. 'Did you say he hadn't yet reached thirty? I took him to be older, around thirty-five.'

Charles smiled this time. 'Rob is twenty-nine—and let that be a lesson to you about high living!'

Laraine looked at a mental picture of Rob, recalling the receding hair from his high forehead, and his look of experience. Thoughtfully, she asked,

'What makes you think he would go for me?'

He lifted a mocking brow. 'My dear girl, I could go for you myself, as you put it, quite easily. Then there's Moira's father, George. He's very attractive and not at all old. he looks even younger than his forty-five years.'

'Really!' Laraine exploded. 'I've had enough! Here, take your beastly jacket and go!'

She made a move to slip his jacket from her shoulders, but was forestalled by his grip on her shoulders from behind, 'You will walk to the house with my jacket where it is if you don't want to catch a chill.'

'Ah, yes,' she cried, not knowing whether to laugh or cry as she felt him propelling her forward, 'I remember you implying that you could have two invalids on your hands, Moira and myself. We mustn't let that happen, must we?'

He dropped his hands and moved beside her to take her upper arm with strong fingers.

'It isn't that at all,' he said coolly. 'You came into the night air after doing a job of massage which was bound to push your temperature up. Had you paused to think about it you would have known that it was a foolhardy thing to do.'

Completely taken aback, and unused to the skill of evasion, Laraine made no effort to free herself from his hold, but she was still tingling with discomfiture when they reached the house. She entered and he followed, closing the door behind him. In the hall she shed his jacket and gave it back to him with an almost inaudible word of thanks. Then he strolled beside her with it flung over one shoulder, looking big and uncaring.

'Incidentally,' he said, 'I appreciate all that you're doing for Moira. I believe she's going to sleep at nights without her usual pill. Also the drawing lessons are a good idea. She certainly needs a hobby to keep her mind occupied.'

They had reached the foot of the stairs and she looked up at him, very slender and graceful in her evening dress.

'I'm not against anything you do for Moira providing you watch your step in regard to any attachments you might make while you are here,' he said quietly. 'At the moment Moira's small world has narrowed down to those immediately around her. Her old friends don't want to know her now that she is an invalid and no fun any more.'

'I understand more than you think.'

A quiver in her voice deepened his quiet regard of her small flushed face, and he added hastily, 'I don't question that, and I know you don't mean to give her cause for distress, but ... things happen sometimes which are beyond one's control ...' He checked himself and added impressively, 'I am still of the opinion that Moira needs a companion who is older and more experienced.' Here his smile quirked his mouth at the corners as his eyes slid over her expression of wide-eyed apprehension. Those eyes, he noticed, were accentuated by the hall lights into a deep golden brown, adding an enchanting piquancy to her face. 'Anyone less fragile-looking and feminine than you I can't imagine.'

'Fortunately you won't have to strain your imagination much longer,' Laraine interrupted him, her low voice shaken, her hands clenched by her sides. 'You'll be able to relax again when we leave for Lochdoone.'

She made a swift move past him and his detaining hand was instantly on her shoulder in a grip which she could not endure any more than she could his company, and she shifted herself free of his touch.

With changing colour she stared at him for a moment before flitting up the stairs, giving him no time for further speech. When she reached her room her limbs were shaking as anger added to the tremors. She recalled Margaret

remarking on Charles' acting out of character since Moira
had come to stay at McGreyfarne, and her anger slowly
receded. He must love the girl so much that, apart from the
frustration he felt at their being kept apart by her present
condition, he was constantly aware of her vulnerability.
And he wanted to ensure that she would not be hurt further.

Later in bed Laraine tried to analyse her feelings towards
Charles McGreyfarne, but it was a hopeless task. Mentally,
she had never felt so confused about a person before. It
seemed impossible that not long ago she had been in
London full of enthusiasm to come north and do what she
could for a helpless girl. She had expected to meet other
people who would no doubt form a small part of her daily
life, but these would be people who would go their own way
and not upset hers unduly. Indeed she would probably
forget their existence when once she had returned to more
familiar surroundings once again. She would never forget
the countryside, the burns gurgling with fresh water and
healthy fish, the pines like sentinels guarding a land of
fantastic unfulfilled beauty all its own. But Charles was
another matter.

Something seemed to be weighing heavily on her chest at
the thought of him and it was a long time before she went
to sleep. During the night her sleep was fitful and at six
o'clock she decided to get up and go in search of the sea. It
was just coming light with a watery sun sleepily on its way
from Norway to warm up the horizon from the east. Going
quietly downstairs after putting on her swimsuit and button-
through dress, Laraine gripped the handles of her beach bag
and looked in on Moira, to find she was still sleeping. She
was closing her door softly when something cold and wet
touched her hand, followed by a warm tongue. Mac was
looking up at her with soulful eyes and glancing intel-
ligently at her beach bag.

'All right,' she whispered, bending down to pat his head.
'You can come—but no sound, mind!'

Putting a finger on her lips, Laraine led him outdoors in

a vain attempt to quell his exuberance as he ran joyfully around her in circles. A warm breeze coming from the west was filled with the numerous scents of summer as they walked down the driveway and out on to the road towards the village. Mac trotted beside her, eyes dancing, pink tongue visible between his strong white teeth as he showed his pleasure at the unexpected treat.

The village church clock chimed half past six as they turned off the road at a sign pointing to the beach. The narrow path led through fields still wet with dew and clumps of gorse turned to silver by the threads of spiders, then across a golf course and on to sand dunes overrun with coarse grass, harebells and green gorse.

And suddenly there was the sea, illuminated by a red-gold sky as the sun rose. It was a moment of pure magic for Laraine, who stood lost in admiration for a while before she began to run down to the beach shouting in her joy. Mac ran before her, scattering seagulls in their search for an early feed, and they reached acres of shimmering beaches turning to gold in the sun. With a sense of freedom Laraine dropped her beach bag, slipped off her button-through dress, then in her swimsuit and bathing cap, she padded over the soft sand to the water's edge.

Mac ran by her side, barking loudly. Once or twice she picked up a stick and threw it into the water for him to fetch back. But this he refused to do; instead he continued to bark frantically as she waded out on the softly flowing tide. This she found very odd. Indeed, he seemed to be almost crying as she struck out strongly.

After the first shock of immersion the water rippled pleasurably over her limbs. Back on the shore Mac was still barking, then she forgot him in the joy of floating on her back and relaxing. She had swum out for some distance when the cold current swirled around her ominously.

It took her breath and chilled her limbs until she was shivering. She turned immediately to swim back to the shore, to find that the current was like an octopus reaching out with indestructible tendrils to hold her prisoner. Desperately she made frantic efforts to reach warmer water, and succeeding at last with a will that exhausted her. To her dismay the shore seemed to be miles away and a feeling of cramp had taken her left leg.

There was a drumming noise in her ears, and it occurred to her that Mac was not barking any more. Too late she realised his reason for not entering the water. He had been warning her of the danger.

'Mac!' she called desperately, with the feeling that his bark would in some idiotic way give her reassurance that she might make it back to the shore. But the only sound to be heard was the soft roll of the waves and the shriek of a seagull somewhere overhead. Laraine turned on to her back and floated for some time to gain her strength and hope for the cramp in her leg to go. But while the water was warmer now she still felt a chill, and the cramp was giving her intense pain. At last she struck out once more for the shore, calling herself all kinds of an idiot for coming so far out.

The effort to swim now was excruciatingly painful, and she gritted her teeth. Gradually the noise in her ears drummed louder and louder until she was hardly conscious of moving. After what seemed like years she was stumbling ashore, the noise in her head becoming more deafening at each step. Her last conscious thought was to get far enough up the beach away from those creeping waves. In the end it did not seem to matter, for something was already wetting her face after she had collapsed face downwards on the sand.

In her dream someone was carrying her through the mists of time and she could again hear Mac's joyful bark as she was lowered on her back. Something soft and comfortable was pushed beneath her head and she opened her eyes. Charles was kneeling beside her and Mac was licking her face excitedly. She tried to struggle up and felt an extraordinary weakness.

'Take it easy,' Charles said gently, and pushed Mac

away. He wore riding clothes and the front of his immaculate jacket was covered with wet sand from carrying her. 'How are you feeling?'

Weakly she answered, 'All kinds of an idiot for swimming out so far from a strange beach. I really thought I'd had it.' She turned to give Mac a look of affection. 'Mac warned me, bless him, but I didn't understand.'

Mac did, however, for he was there, kissing her again, making her face sticky with his licking.

Charles said sternly, 'Stop it, Mac!' and his voice sounded unusually thick. Mac sat down obediently a few feet away to survey them both with dancing eyes and lolling tongue, and he snuggled up against Charles, who sat down now on the sand beside her. 'Why on earth didn't you mention that you might go down to the beach?' he went on. 'Had you come during the day you would have seen this part was deserted. Not only is it dangerous to bathe here, it's also inaccessible by car.'

Laraine lay back against the pillow he had pushed beneath her head. She presumed that it was her button-through dress and longed to put it on to cover her scantily clad form. With anyone else it would not have mattered so much, but Charles made her too aware of being undressed. At the moment she was too spent even too move. Her breath still hurt in her chest and she felt lethargic and uncaring.

Words tumbled out. 'I would have been fine, only I had cramp in my left leg,' she confessed. 'It was dreadful.'

He dusted the wet sand clinging to her slim brown legs and his fingers moved over her left foot in a circular movement until she felt a certain amount of relief. Then he was massaging her leg behind the knee and she sat up to find the cramp had gone.

'Thanks,' she said with a more normal feeling flooding through her. 'How did you know I was here, and how did you come so quickly?'

'Mac,' he said laconically. 'He came pelting into the

house at top speed to tell me that something was amiss, so I came on Blacky with Mac leading the way.'

Laraine followed his gaze to where a horse stood patiently waiting and nibbling the coarse grass not far away. She fumbled behind for her dress and instantly Charles was on his feet helping her to put it on.

'I'm sorry to cause you this trouble . . .' she began, fastening the last button and bending to pick up her beach bag.

In looking up at him she was aware of a sense of confusion. It seemed he had an upsetting way of making her feel conscious of him with relation to herself. It worried her, this disconcerting thing that flared up between them as though it was something intimately personal. Yet he did not appear to be aware of it. In fact he was so unaware of it that she felt a resentful urge to jolt him out of his cool.

'That's all right,' he answered. 'No harm has been done. I won't say you enjoyed such an unpleasant experience, but you'll be none the worse for it.'

He knelt down after taking the sandals she had taken from the beach bag to put on her feet. Dusting the sand from her soles, he took a look at the cut beneath her foot before slipping on the sandals.

'The adhesive dressing is off. I'll see to it when we get back to the house. There could be some sand in it.'

Laraine paused for a moment, about to tell him that she would see to it herself, then decided against it as being petty since he had come to her assistance. In any case it would do no good to argue with him since it would inevitably end in a loss of dignity for her and would also make things very uncomfortable between them. So she accepted his hand and let him pull her to her feet. Inwardly she was aware of his former belief that she would only bring trouble, and it seemed to her in that inflated moment that he had been right.

'Ready?' he asked, and they walked to where his horse was waiting.

He mounted her first, then swung up easily behind her.

Mac trotted beside them and they made their way back to McGreyfarne.

After Laraine had had a bath and dressed, she had, on Charles' instructions, gone along the corridor to a bathroom at the far end where he had cleaned the cut on her foot and dressed it.

'It's healing nicely,' he observed.

She sat on a bath stool and he knelt beside her with her foot in his hand. His face was almost expressionless, his eyes impenetrable. She nodded voicelessly as she watched him apply the waterproof dressing. His fair head was very near and there was a heart-shaking moment when she felt the urge to touch the springy hair. She could understand any woman falling for his charm, and the fugitive thought passed through her mind that many had.

Retaining her foot in his warm grip, he said sardonically, 'Nice golden tan you have. Did you acquire it on some tycoon's yacht?'

Laraine felt her nerves tighten at his tone. She followed his eyes down to her long slim golden legs and said quietly, 'No. I used to sunbathe during the lunch hour on the roof of the block of offices where I worked.'

'I see,' laconically.

He released her foot and she drew it away nervously. 'Thank you,' she said simply. The atmosphere seemed to have become charged with an indefinable significance. Then Charles stood up abruptly.

'Take care of it, especially if you go swimming. Put on a new dressing each day, won't you?' he said.

He had gone before Laraine could reply.

He was not there for breakfast, but Margaret joined her to say that they were all going to a garden party that afternoon at the manse. So after a morning spent on a painting session with Moira, they all set out for the manse.

It was a perfect day for a garden party with the sun shining in a clear blue sky. There were stalls, sideshows and games on the lawns, followed by a tea country style with everything grown locally and nothing out of a can or freezer except the ice cream. All the village appeared to have turned out for it, including Rob McIndle, who seemed so pleased to see her. Like Charles, he wore a kilt charmingly.

It would not have been natural for Laraine not to have felt a little flattered by his attentions. Margaret was presiding on the committee seeing to everything, and Moira was taking part in an archery competition with Charles when Laraine left them to stroll with Rob and take tea with him on two secluded seats in the rockery of the manse.

'This is lovely,' she said with shining eyes. 'Fare for the gods!'

She bit into home-made pastry filled with fresh fruit and wrinkled her nose at him deliciously.

He drank some of his tea and smiled at her appraisingly. 'That's what I like about you,' he murmured, bending forward in a teasing, friendly manner. 'You're so natural, and you find your enjoyment in simple things. I ought to have met you years ago.'

'You mean before you lost your money? I doubt if I would have made any difference to you. And money isn't everything.'

'I suppose it isn't when you're young and can work for it. There's a sense of values in it as well.' He took down the rest of his tea and gazed unseeingly into the rockery around them. 'Did you know that once Moira and I were more or less engaged?'

Laraine's eyes widened. 'No, I didn't know,' she exclaimed in surprise. 'What happened?'

He shrugged. 'Well, we grew up together. You could say it has something to do with a sense of values. We're both the product of fond doting parents ... thought the world was our oyster. We just lived it up, went everywhere and joined in everything until my money ran out.'

'I'm sorry,' she said gently.

'Nothing to be sorry about. It just didn't work out. Moira's father was very decent about it. He engaged me to manage his estate at a fairly good salary. I work now and I like it.'

'And your parents?'

'My father died and Mother married again. She's now in Canada, the wife of a cattle baron.'

Laraine said on an afterthought, 'Why not go out there to better prospects?'

'I've thought about it, but something keeps me here.'

'Moira?' she asked.

'You could say that. Her father has been decent to me and Moira needs all the friends she can get at the moment.'

'She might walk again.'

Rob shrugged. 'And she might not.'

'That's a defeatist attitude,' Laraine said firmly.

He grinned. 'You see, like I said, I ought to have met you years ago.'

To Laraine he sounded pathetic and not at all like a young man should be, full of fight and vigour. He was looking rather drawn about his cheekbones as though he had not slept. She could guess what had happened. When his money had gone Moira had left him for fresh fields to have fun. She had gone to London joined a fast set and then the accident had happened.

The tragedy must have come when Rob was picking himself up after finding himself broke, so he had suffered a double blow. It was only natural that his feelings for Moira, a childhood sweetheart, should still be deep inside him. And Moira had not shown any particular feeling for Rob, unless she was taking him for granted along with her father.

Laraine did not relish the thought of becoming too deeply involved, and found herself wishing fervently for Moira's father to return; only then would she feel as if she was getting somewhere regarding his daughter.

Rob lighted a cigarette, blew out a line of smoke and said, 'How are you liking it here? Rather quiet after London. I think it's very brave of you to come.' He looked frankly at her. 'Moira has always preferred the company of men, but I'm sure you'll be good for her.'

Laraine sipped her tea. 'Thanks. Nice to know that you don't think I have an ulterior motive for coming.'

He raised a brow. 'Why should I? By the way, I had no idea that you were involved in Moira's accident until you said so the first evening we met at McGreyfarne. I believe the man who ran her down was a millionaire.'

Laraine laughed. 'Not quite. He was a friend of mine whom I met through one of my best friends. We met at her wedding.'

'Very romantic. Why didn't you hook him?'

Laraine said diplomatically, 'It didn't work out that way.'

'I bet you refused him. No man in his right mind would turn a blind eye to you.'

She laughed again. 'Do you know, I shall be getting suspicious that you want something from me just now. Why so nice?'

'Because you are nice. Hasn't anyone ever told you?'

'Not on so short acquaintance—but it's very nice all the same!'

They were smiling at each other when Charles appeared with Moira in her wheelchair. 'So this is where you are,' he said. His glance, keen and enigmatic, slid from Laraine to Rob, whom he continued to address. 'Perhaps you'll see to some refreshment for Moira. I have to distribute the prizes with the vicar.'

Moira was annoyed. 'Why didn't you stop for the archery, Laraine?' she demanded harshly. 'You could have taken part.'

Laraine's face grew hot beneath her anger, she felt it as a distinct rebuke on Moira's part. 'Sorry, I didn't want to intrude,' she said.

'You mean you wanted to be with Rob? Is that why you didn't take part, Rob? You always have taken part before,' Moira accused him.

He lifted careless shoulders. 'I thought I'd sit that one out since you had Charles with you.' He grinned at her and rose lazily to his feet. 'What's the matter, darling? Do you want us both? Not jealous, by any chance, are you?'

He patted the top of her head as he passed her wheelchair and Moira moved her head angrily to one side as he did so.

'Sometimes I hate you, Rob McIndle,' she said tightly through clenched teeth.

Laraine watched him go with dismay and tried to appease her companion.

'What about going to see Charles present the prizes?' she suggested gently. 'Then you could have your tea on the terrace.'

'Stop treating me like an idiot!' Moira hissed, gripping the arms of her chair and shaking it. 'If only I could get out of this thing!'

Helplessly Laraine watched tears of weakness fall from her eyes, and when Rob returned with a tray she slipped quietly away, leaving them together. Wandering around the stalls, she had a word with Margaret, then looked for Charles. He was on the terrace standing in front of a table containing various prizes for the events ranging from small cups to bottles of wine, perfume, boxes of chocolates, cigars, groceries, etc.

He performed the task of handing out the prizes with his usual charm, assisted by the vicar, who read the names of winners from a list in his hand. When a pretty teenager came forward to collect her prize she tiptoed to kiss Charles, much to the amusement of the crowd. The women booed in mock jealousy and the men wolf-whistled. Charles grinned, looking big and uncaring in his kilt. At last all the prizes had been presented with the exception of one, a beauty box of make-up. There was obviously a prize too many, and seeing it left on the table gave Laraine an idea.

Charles was leaving the terrace when she stepped forward.

'Please may I speak to you for a moment?' she said.

'Is anything the matter?' he asked, drawing her aside.

The crowd was melting away and she said in a low voice, 'Did Moira score at the archery this afternoon?'

'As a matter of fact she did. Unfortunately she just missed the second prize. Why?'

Under his intent gaze her cheeks flamed. 'Well, seeing that prize left on the table gave me an idea. Surely you could give it to her? I've just left her and she's terribly depressed. It would be a nice gesture, and you could present it as a third prize for archery.'

He looked down for a long time into her earnest face, then strode to where the vicar was talking with several of his parishioners near the terrace. Minutes later he was back with the beauty box.

'That was a nice thought,' he said. 'I take it that you don't want Moira to know that you suggested it?'

Laraine looked horrified. 'Good heavens, no,' she cried. 'That's the whole point. Moira must think she's won it. We have to make her interested in things that will take her mind off herself. This prize will be so good for her morale and she'll have endless fun with it using the different make-up. She'll love it. Don't you see?'

Her eyes in her delicately boned small face sparkled with enthusiasm, and in her excitement she laid a hand on his arm. Her head was tilted a little to one side as she waited for him to speak. In that moment her eyes met his in a sudden tingling sense of shock. The colour rushed to her face and she drew her hand from his arm quickly as if it stung.

'I'm beginning to,' he drawled.

Laraine blinked, waited until her treacherous heart had righted itself and said hurriedly, 'I ... I think it will be better if you go on ahead. That way Moira will never doubt that she's won a prize.'

Charles stood quietly looking down at her for several moments, seemed about to speak, then turned on his heel and strode away. Watching him, Laraine felt in need of support. Her heart was beating in thick strokes and was threatening to choke her. What an idiot she was, to let him upset her so. Yet it seemed incredible that he had not felt the same sense of shock when their eyes had locked just now. She certainly would have to see that psychiatrist, since all the emotion invoked seemed to be on her side.

When she eventually joined them in the rockery, Charles was standing beside Moira's wheelchair with Rob on the other side. They were both grinning down at her flushed face as she held the beauty box. Rob was the first to speak at her approach.

'Come and see what Moira's won, Laraine,' he said. 'Seems we should have had a go at that archery after all.'

'Isn't it wonderful?' Moira was evidently thrilled with the prize, and Laraine knew they had done the right thing. She met Charles' mocking gaze above Moira's head and looked quickly away again, aware that the girl was talking. 'I owe you an apology, Laraine,' she said. 'I can see now why you suggested me going to see Charles hand over the prizes—you actually thought there might have been one for me. I'm sorry I was so rude to you.'

Laraine, filled with compassion, said gently, 'I'm glad you did so well. You don't know what you can do until you try. Anyway, there's no excuse now for not making yourself look beautiful.'

Moira nodded. 'I'm glad you came, Laraine,' she said simply.

CHAPTER FIVE

SINCE the garden party Moira had come down to breakfast each morning and she appeared to have regained a normal appetite. The colour returned to her cheeks and her enthusiasm over the painting lessons increased. Laraine, encouraged by her co-operation, was careful not to spoil her by giving in to her imperious demands. Used to having her own way, she could be overbearing at times. When she was being unusually fractious, Laraine would produce the first sketch that she had done of her which Moira had kept as a reminder of her sulky expression and hold it up silently for her to see. The action usually produced giggles on both sides, and Moira's good humour was restored.

As for Charles, he insisted upon keeping his distance where Laraine was concerned. Even the little secret between them regarding the beauty box had not brought him any closer. At first Laraine had been hurt, but now she had wisely learned to accept it. His behaviour to Moira was very different. He was in turn gentle, teasing and mocking, and was even given to kissing her on the occasions when she took the initiative.

Witnessing those kisses, Laraine had been shattered at the deep emotion she had felt. Jealousy, she discovered for the first time in her life, was shatteringly painful. It told her that she was falling in love with him against her better judgment. Helplessly she felt the emanation of herself being slowly and irrevocably assimilated by a big uncaring Scotsman who, at times, seemed totally unaware of her existence.

But if she had grown farther away from Charles, she had grown nearer to Margaret, who never ceased to thank her for what she had done for her dear Moira. It was Margaret

71

who suggested giving a party now that Moira's health had improved. There was to be a bar, and long tables set out Swedish style, and heavily laden with endless dishes, salads, sandwiches, vol-au-vents filled with delicious concoctions, shellfish and all kinds of things—not forgetting the haggis! A band of pipers and Highland dancers had been engaged and fairy lights were put up among the trees in the grounds.

It was impossible to count the number of guests who arrived, bringing with them an air of sophistication and good breeding. Most of the men wore kilts and the women were beautifully dressed. Charles looked hearbreakingly handsome in his kilt which seemed to enhance his wide-shouldered, virile figure. He greeted his guests cordially and it was easy to see that the parties at McGreyfarne were very popular. Upon the arrival of the last guests, Moira had propelled her wheelchair forward and taken Charles' hand in her own in a careless, happy gesture indicative of an indulged girl claiming the attention of the one man in her life. And to Laraine it seemed that Charles was quite happy about it.

She had looked away hastily for someone she knew, but they were all strangers to her. It occurred to her then to look for the comforting presence of Rob, but he did not appear to have come. She was about to join Margaret whom she had sighted across the room when Morag tapped her on the shoulder.

'Excuse me, lassie,' she said. 'You're wanted in the library.'

Minutes later Laraine was entering a room of booklined walls and comfortable well-used leather easy chairs. The knowledge that it was Charles' sanctum set up all manner of vibrations inside her. But it was not Charles who waited with his back to the fireplace in order to see her enter.

The man striding across the room to greet her was a stranger. He was of medium height, slightly built and rather dapper in a dark city-going suit which he evidently had not had time to change. His neat brown hair was well brushed and his long sensitive face held a strange attraction. But he looked tired and drawn as if he had not been sleeping well.

'Good evening,' he said with a twinkle. 'Miss Laraine Winters?'

He held out his hand and she put hers into it, watching the fine network of wrinkles around his eyes which his smile brought into play.

'Yes,' she answered with a smile. 'You're Moira's father?'

He nodded. 'Shall we sit down?' He led the way to two easy chairs by the fireplace. 'I must apologise for taking you away from the party, but I wanted a word with you about Moira before I make my presence known.' He hitched up his trousers by the crease and sat down facing her. 'My daughter was against having a companion, but I thought that someone around her own age would be good for her. This is a terrible thing that's happened, and I must say she's taking it much better since you arrived. I can't tell you how grateful I am that you've come. An older woman might have been more pessimistic and fuss her too much. Tell me, what do you think about her?'

Laraine wrinkled a smooth brow. 'You mean her present condition, of course?'

He nodded, adding hurriedly, 'I've had reports from Margaret—Miss McGreyfarne—and I've also received a rather reserved account from Moira, but I want to know what you think.'

Laraine bit her lip. The man was obviously very concerned about his daughter and she wanted to help him.

'When I came,' she began, 'Moira was not eating or sleeping well, so her health was below par. Now she's not only sleeping without a pill, she's also eating again quite well. So naturally she has improved a lot.' She leaned forward earnestly. 'It's possible for her to walk again some day, that I do believe, but it's getting her to believe it too.

You see, her health had deteriorated through not eating or sleeping well and she'd lost interest in everything—and that included her own recovery.'

He nodded in agreement. 'Moira flatly refused to go away for treatment. Perhaps I'm partly to blame for that because I've always given in to her every whim. In fact if I hadn't given her permission to go to live in London after her break with Rob McIndle this would never have happened. You've met Rob?'

'Yes.'

'He could have been different had he not been as spoiled as my daughter. The best thing that could have happened to him was his mother's second marriage. It ended the influence she had on him, but by then he had squandered away his inheritance. Anyway, I have faith in the boy, that's why I took him on as my estate manager.'

'And you think Charles McGreyfarne is a better influence on your daughter?'

He laughed. 'Yes, I do. In fact I'm hoping that everything will work out for Moira so that they can marry. It would solve one problem.'

Laraine wondered if he meant the problem of marrying Margaret once Moira was off his hands. She was sure they would marry given the chance, and after meeting this delightful man, she could not wait for it to happen. After all, when Charles was married to Moira she would be on her way out of their lives.

Determined to be cheerful, she said, 'Your daughter mentioned that you'd gone to Rome to see someone who might help her recover the use of her limbs. May I ask if you had any satisfaction from him?'

'In a way,' he admitted. 'Naturally Moira would have to go and see him.' He consulted his watch and gave an exclamation of dismay. 'Heavens, I'm spoiling your party! It seems that I've spoiled Rob's as well, since he came to meet me. He's gone on to Lochdoone with my luggage. How do you feel about leaving McGreyfarne for Lochdoone?'

She smiled. 'I shall be sorry to leave Margaret. She's so sweet.'

Good heavens, she thought, the man's blushing!—and just then Margaret herself tapped on the door and entered. Her delight on seeing George Frazer illuminated her face before she had time to control her surprise and pleasure. Laraine murmured something and slipped hurriedly from the room, leaving them together.

The piper band struck up a lively tune as she made her way to the room where all the guests were gathered. At the door she peered in to see the pipers in full regalia circling the centre of the floor before forming a circle around the cleared space to make way for the dancers. They were very good, dancing over crossed swords, and receiving loud applause.

When the dancing display ended the dancers drew the guests forward to join in the dancing. From her place just inside the door of the room Laraine saw Moira at the far end with Charles, and her heart went out to the girl because she was unable to join in the fun. Then Margaret had joined them, presumably to tell them of George Frazer's arrival. Laraine looked at Charles while a pang sweet, tremulous and aching, washed over her, then she turned swiftly and crossed the hall.

Fairy lights twinkled among the trees in the grounds and the sweet night air was a mixture of honeysuckle and the tang of the sea. Laraine took several deep breaths gratefully and tried to relax. All right, she was being very foolish to allow Charles to upset her so much. She ought to be used to his presence by now, but she doubted whether she ever would be. It was something she had to fight.

All she wanted was to get through the time she remained at McGreyfarne without betraying her feelings for him, to exchange such civilities as politeness demanded and leave with Moira in the shortest possible time to Lochdoone. It was impossible to remain in his vicinity for long without betraying her love for him, he stirred her physically too much.

Once at Lochdoone things would be different. At the moment she had singularly little to do for Moira with Charles around. Whenever he appeared she felt bound to leave them together because she was sure that was what Moira wanted. And there was Margaret also waiting to help whenever she could where Moira was concerned.

It was some time since Margaret had told Moira that her father had arrived and they were by now meeting him in the library. Laraine knew that she ought to go in to join them, but she lingered in the sweet night air to listen to the music from the pipe band. She saw the headlights first as they pierced the fading light, then the car was coming up the drive to the door.

It was Rob McIndle come to fetch his employer home. Leaving the car, he strode across to her with obvious pleasure.

'Looking for me?' he asked teasingly in greeting, and lifted a hand. 'No, don't say you weren't, let me delude myself that you were. I expect George has made my apologies for not arriving earlier.'

Laraine nodded, pleased to see him. 'He told me about it. Anyway, the evening isn't over yet. I think you will find them all in the library. I was thinking of going to join them in case it's expected of me. After all, I'm only an employee like you.'

'But that doesn't mean that you and I can't snatch a few moments from time to time to enjoy ourselves. What about us joining in the dance? Come on, I refuse to take no for an answer!'

Before she could reply he had taken her arm and was marching her indoors. For the next half hour she thoroughly enjoyed herself as Rob took her through all the traditional Scottish dances. Her face was flushed and her breath was coming and going deliciously in audible rhythm. Rob had changed into his kilt, and he proved an agile dancer and an excellent teacher.

'Sure you haven't done this kind of thing before?' he asked, twirling her around as she looked up laughing at him. 'You're as light as a bit of thistledown and I can see the envy of the males around us. You're making quite an impression on them.'

She chuckled, loving his foolery. 'Stop making absurd remarks,' she said. 'If anyone is looking at us they're perhaps wondering what on earth I'm doing dancing with you in the first place. I suppose like everywhere else this corner of the world is not immune to gossip.'

'We have our moments,' he admitted with a grin. 'What about us taking some refreshment? I'd like a drink. How about a tomato juice and haggis?'

Laraine wrinkled her nose in alarm. 'Sounds disgusting together—but I'll try it!'

'Bravely spoken!' Rob offered her his arm gallantly as the music stopped for an interval and led her to the improvised tables and bar.

'But shouldn't we be looking for our respective employers?' she asked tentatively.

He shrugged. 'They'll send someone to find us if they want us.'

They had their tomato juice and amidst much laughing Rob offered her a sample of the haggis on a fork.

'Close your eyes, open your mouth, then chew,' he advised with a grin.

Solemnly Laraine did so. 'Hmm, it isn't bad at all. In fact I could acquire a taste for it,' she said. 'Thanks.'

'Don't mention it,' he answered, and they both giggled.

They had been standing at a corner of the bar with Jock finding time in between attending to demands for drinks to smile on them benignly. Laraine had secretly blessed him for not raising a quizzical brow at them having fun. She was almost sure that Charles would not approve. And suddenly there he was.

'So you've arrived, Rob,' he said. 'You're wanted in the library. I'll bring Laraine along.'

He was smiling when he spoke, but it was the wrong kind

of smile. Before Laraine could say anything Rob had finished his drink and left them.

Glancing up at his closed expression, she wanted to
follow Rob and leave him, but his hand was on her arm.

'I want to talk to you,' he said coldly. 'Shall we walk?'

His fingers were on her elbow lightly and he led her from
the room. Looking up at his clear-cut profile Laraine
caught herself thinking, I wish he would treat me just once
as a friend. Aloud she said, 'Have I to pack my things? Are
we returning this evening to Lochdoone now that Mr
Frazer has returned?'

'Nothing has been said about it. I would say you'll be
leaving tomorrow at the very earliest,' he answered in that
cool voice. His eyes were fixed upon her, on her body lithe
and slender in the simple evening gown, her hair rioting in
damp tendrils about her face and the warm glow in her
cheeks. Then surprisingly he asked, 'What do you think of
Moira's father?'

He had escorted her to the door of the room with his easy
masterful stride. His height, the wide shoulders, his overwhelming presence seemed to shrivel her up into a mindless
fool. Desperately she decided on a counter-attack.

'I'm sure that isn't the reason why we're dawdling behind
Rob,' she said quietly.

They had reached the hall and in the subdued quiet the
atmosphere seemed to be charged with an undercurrent.
She drew away from him with a coolness that matched his
and waited.

'It was one of the reasons,' he prevaricated.

'Then I'd better tell you, since I'm sure the other reasons
could be unpleasant. He's a most charming man and I'm
looking forward to going to Lochdoone.'

'I'm sure you are,' he jibed cynically, 'since Rob Mc-
Indle will be there.'

'That's a rotten thing to say!' She clenched her hands by
her sides and looked up at him with blazing eyes. 'I know
you can't bear to see me having a good time for some reason
or other, but fortunately you won't have to endure it much

longer. I might as well tell you that had you employed me instead of Mr Frazer, I wouldn't have stayed here another minute. As far as I can see what I or Rob McIndle do is no business of yours.'

She choked on the last word, finding it impossible to say more. Emotions crowded in on her, and emotions were very dangerous when Charles was about. Furthermore, she had lost her temper with him, which was not a wise thing to do. It was a state of mind that he could take advantage of by tying it into knots. What was the matter with the man? He couldn't possibly be jealous. Then it occurred to her that he did not want Moira hurt. Moira's welfare was his only concern, and his next words corroborated this.

He said curtly, 'You have admitted coming here to help Moira. Then show that you mean it by keeping your distance with her father and with Rob. I admit what I saw just now was just a little harmless fun between you, but it could very easily flare up into something much deeper. You've done good work with her up to now—don't ruin it all by thoughtlessness.'

'If you're so concerned about her why don't you marry her yourself, to give her all the reassurance she needs? You could even take her to Rome on your honeymoon to see the surgeon there!'

Laraine had spoken with sudden heat again. Holding herself in check with him was something she was finding impossible. But the moment the words were out she regretted them. Too late she was aware of interfering in what was not her business. She saw him go a trifle pale around the nostrils beneath his tan, and knew she had at last got beneath his guard. She stared confounded at the dark face so tightly set that for one horrible instant she was afraid. Never in her life had she acted so impulsively.

Anger slowly left her, pushed away by a sense of having trespassed upon someone else's private affairs. These things did not happen to her, were not of her world. What could she possibly say?

She could only say with painful hesitancy, 'I'm sorry, I

shouldn't have said that. It was rude and unforgivable ...
and ... and very presumptuous of me.'

She saw the gold of his hair muted in the hall lights, the
strong lines of the Celt in his high cheekbones as his very
withdrawal gave her the feeling of an utter stranger.

Then he said coldly, 'Shall we go to the library?'

Much later, back in her room after giving Moira a last-
minute massage, Laraine sat in front of her dressing table
mirror patting face cream on to her skin. They were to leave
for Lochdoone the following morning. It had come at last,
the break she needed from Charles. But did she want it?
The thought of him made her hands tremble. She wanted
him, in spite of all the scorn she had poured upon herself.
Wanted him so much that nothing else mattered. And it
was all so hopeless.

Moira did not really need her either. Sooner or later she
would have come round to her father's way of thinking and
gone to Rome for the specialist there to help her to a complete recovery. Charles with his keen insight had seen that,
but he had no idea that she would be foolish enough to fall
in love with him. It was something he must never know.
But she had a goal—to do what was right—and she would
do it if it killed her.

CHAPTER SIX

THEY left for Lochdoone the following morning with Rob coming to fetch them in the estate car. He carried Moira to the front seat beside him and Laraine went in the back with the wheelchair and the luggage. Charles was not there to see them go. He was out on the estate.

They all gave a cheery wave to Margaret and the car swept down the drive, then on towards the village. Laraine looked through the window in case Charles was somewhere around, but they swept on through the village without a sign of him. Houses became few and far between and they were climbing upwards towards thick pines. The air was now filled with the quality of country smells—honeysuckle, thyme and the resinous scent of pine. The latter stood out against the blue of the sky, then the wheels were turning to the left to crunch on the gravel of a drive.

And there it was, Lochdoone, not a large house, not even as large as McGreyfarne, but dignified and homely. There was a terrace backed by tall windows leading out on to well planned grounds. It was two-storied with a bell tower to give it dignity, a grey pile of stone built to last through generations of bad times and good.

Laraine was not disappointed as they swung round to pull up silently at the front door. There was nothing about it to give her qualms about living there. In fact her spirits lifted as Rob came to lift out the wheelchair and carry it indoors. Then he came for Moira. As he carried her into the house Laraine followed.

The hall was bathed in golden light from high windows bringing to life the panelled walls and beautiful curving staircase which confronted one on entering. To the right of the staircase was a lift, put in no doubt for Moira. George

Frazer came lightly down the stairs as Rob seated his daughter in the wheelchair.

'Welcome home, darling,' he said, bending down to kiss her.

Moira put her arms around his neck as Rob went out to collect the luggage.

'What have you brought me?' she demanded, like an indulged child.

'Your present is in your room, darling,' her father said fondly, and patted the top of her head as he released her.

Laraine had looked away at their greeting and fixed her eyes on a lustre bowl of roses in an arched alcove in the hall. Fleetingly she was thinking that Moira might at the moment need all the love and care she could get, but the sort of indulgent care her father gave her was hardly the kind to do the girl most good. So it was with a mixture of amusement and compassion that she watched her propel her wheelchair across the hall to the lift.

'She'll be all right on her own.' George Frazer had put out a hand on Laraine's arm when she had made to follow. 'I want you to meet the staff,' he told her with a smile. 'We have a woman who comes in daily from the village and a resident housekeeper with her husband. Here's Mrs Dougal now.'

A woman had entered the hall from one of the doors to the left of the staircase. She was motherly but smart and about forty-five. Her glance at Laraine was curious but kind as she came forward with a smile which showed good teeth. George introduced them both and was told that Dougal was in the village fetching in supplies.

Laraine was following the housekeeper upstairs when Rob passed them after taking the luggage to her room. His friendly grin did much to make her feel at home.

Her room was next to Moira's along a pleasant corridor brightened by arrangements of flowers in alcoves. It was light and airy with a large bed both springy and comfortable and dark furniture enlivened by printed linen covers.

The adjoining bathroom was in chrome and primrose with big fluffy towels and perfumed soap.

Deciding to leave her unpacking until later, Laraine ran a comb through her hair, wiped her face with a powder puff, and shaking off the feeling of being a stranger in a strange house, went to Moira's room. Unlike her own it was rich in décor. The walls were papered in a delicate pink and grey stripe, the bed canopied in lace. Brightly coloured lamps and cushions were scattered around, their colours blending with the flower arrangements and rugs. On the exquisite white lace bedspread with its underlining of pink satin was a gorgeous array of negligé, obviously from the fashion houses of Rome. There were also expensive leather goods, Italian hand-made shoes, gloves and hand-bags along with other gee-gaws which every girl loves, lavish gifts from a fond father.

Moira was at the dressing table mirror trying on a neck-lace of crystal. She spun her wheelchair round as Laraine entered.

'Like it?' she asked, her eyes shining with pleasure.

'Yes. It's very pretty.'

Laraine walked across the thick pile carpet thinking that here was a girl who had so much, yet so little. She was a caged bird who could have practically everything she wanted except freedom. Her eyes shied away from the pulley at the side of the bed, so incongruous in such a pretty room.

Poor Moira, she thought, wrapped in a cocoon of love and indulgence until tragedy had struck. She simply was not built to cope with it. Laraine wanted to help, and she did pity her; even more she pitied her father. A widower for years, he must have been very lonely at times, but he had sacrificed his own happiness for his daughter.

They spent some time gloating over the gifts and Laraine wrapped them in tissue paper to put them away. But before the task was complete it was obvious that Moira had lost interest. She was polishing her nails with an air of detachment which irritated.

Laraine said carefully as she straightened the bedspread to its former neatness, 'Your father is impressed by the man in Rome who he thinks can help you to walk again.'

'Daddy has been impressed before by these men who think they're God. I'm not, that's all.'

'Just the same, you wouldn't lose anything by going. I know you're coping very well, but you won't have much privacy. You really want someone with you most of the time in case of accidents.'

Moira shook her lovely head impatiently. 'I refuse to go over all that again. Being prodded and used like a guinea-pig hasn't done anything for me up to now. Besides, I was never a sporty type. I love being fussed over and coddled. And I have Charles.' Her eyes grew dreamy. 'Do you know, he never used to bother with me, but since the accident he can't do enough for me. And I have you.'

Laraine knew the last four words had been meant to provoke. She could dismiss them lightheartedly, but not the implication.

She said frankly, 'I haven't come to stay with you indefinitely. I came because I want you to walk again. I also came to help you make life more bearable and get you back to health.'

'I am back to health. Now what do I do, get up and walk?'

Laraine swept up a piece of tissue paper from the carpet and folded it neatly. 'I don't think that's very funny, and I'm sure you don't either.'

'Don't tell me it worries you?'

'Yes, it does. After all, I'm here to help, and believe me, I want to very much.'

Moira laughed, but her eyes didn't. 'I find that very funny.'

'Have it your own way,' Laraine answered resignedly. 'You always will. The trouble is that sometimes you're your own worst enemy.'

Moira looked unrepentent. 'All right, you've had your say. Now let's drop the matter, shall we? I think it's time for coffee.' She consulted the small exquisite wrist watch, and added, 'Ring for Mrs Dougal.'

Laraine hesitated, then looked her right in the eye. 'Don't you think it would be nice to go downstairs and have it with your father? There's so much you have to talk about, and you have to thank him for the lovely and generous gifts.'

Moira sneered openly, 'You think of everything, don't you?'

'No, I don't, but it's nice to think of other people once in a while.'

George Frazer was alone in the dining room when Laraine went down the next morning. He wore slacks and a velvet smoking jacket with a cravat tucked in at the neck. He looked like a country squire and his easy smile put her immediately at her ease.

Uncertain what to wear herself, she had decided on slacks and a cashmere top, thinking it would make her look workmanlike and capable of looking after Moira. The fact that she was a hundred per cent feminine and looked it was something that she was aware of since taking the post as Moira's companion. Before, her fragile appearance hadn't bothered her unduly.

'I've looked in on Moira,' she said as he seated her at the table. 'She's still asleep.'

'And likely to be for another hour at least,' said Moira's fond father. 'Moira has never enjoyed rising too early in the morning. Most young things don't these days. In fact they take pleasure in not doing any of the things I did in my youth—but there it is. Did you sleep well?'

'Yes, thanks.' Laraine turned to smile at the big man who entered with a laden tray which he emptied on to the sideboard behind her.

George said, 'Dougal, this is Miss Laraine Winters who has come as a companion for Moira.'

Dougal stood hesitatingly beside her chair and Laraine smilingly offered a hand which he took. He had fiery red hair and his face was almost as red as he greeted her.

George chuckled. 'Dougal is going to love feeding you up, Laraine, so woe betide you if you don't make a good breakfast!'

She laughed and her eyes danced at the red-haired brawny Scot, who was now looking at his ease.

She said demurely, 'One thing I've never done is pick at my food. But don't expect me to put on weight, because I never do.'

George said darkly, 'Don't you believe it. Before Dougal's done with you we shall have you tossing the caber before you know where you are.'

Laraine laughed outright at this, then sobered when she saw the amount of food Dougal was putting on her plate. To her surprise she ate it and enjoyed the change of food. They talked during the meal mainly about Moira. Laraine learned a lot about her likes and dislikes and tried to put herself in the other girl's place. But her compassion was not as strong as it had been because she felt that Moira was not really trying to be as co-operative as she might.

As for her father, Laraine did not like the lines around his eyes and almost permanent crease in his forehead as if he was worrying himself to death about his daughter. He could have made the trip to Rome as part of a holiday, but she could just imagine him chafing to be back. After breakfast she left him at the table going through his mail and she collided with something in the hall.

'Hey now, not so fast! Where's the fire?'

Charles had grabbed her by the arms to help her to keep her balance. He was laughing down into her face, affable, charming, as if pleased to see her. Laraine stared and wanted to say, 'This is Laraine, remember, the girl you don't like.' Instead it took her all her time to gather her wits. If only he had been like this from the beginning, it would have been easier then to relax in his presence.

'Sorry,' she said. 'Moira is in her room. I'll tell her.'

'Thanks,' he drawled, 'but I've come to see her father. How's the foot?'

His hands still rested on her arms, sending all kinds of vibrations through her. For a moment she looked blank.

'Oh, you mean the cut? It's healed nicely, thanks.'

There was a silence as his arms dropped away from her. Laraine did not care for his probing look. Also he had taken her at a disadvantage, for which she blamed him unfairly.

A little on her dignity, she said, 'Mr Frazer is in the dining room. He's just had breakfast.'

He straightened and looked down mockingly on her flushed face.

'I presume you shared it with him. What was it like—cosy?'

Her chin lifted and anger sparkled in her eyes. 'Why, how did you know, Mr McGreyfarne?' she asked, using his last name deliberately. 'It certainly was, and I can't wait to repeat it.'

'I bet you can't. Well, he's a better proposition than Rob. Things working out all right for you, are they?'

Laraine could never swear afterwards that it was her hand that delivered the stinging slap to his taunting face. The sharp sound seemed to echo all over the house, and the next moment she was running upstairs.

Charles did not stay to lunch. Evidently his business with Moira's father was short. He had seen Moira before he left for she had gone down to join him and her father for mid-morning coffee. Laraine had remained upstairs packing painting equipment for them to go out that afternoon. At lunch she learned from George that Charles and Margaret were coming to dine with them that evening. It was a kind of thank-you on his part for what they had done for his daughter while he had been away.

The thought of meeting Charles again that evening spoiled Laraine's afternoon. At George's suggestion she had taken the station wagon with a drop down at the back for Moira to enter in her wheelchair, and driven out to a glen leading down to the sea. One of the stipulations on applying for the job had been that she could drive. There was a rare beauty about the glen with the water cascading down beneath small rustic bridges on its way to the sea. Like all countries steeped in history it had an air of assurance and inspiration about it.

Leaving the station wagon on the road, she wheeled Moira down the path of the glen and on to a rustic bridge where she set up the easels for painting the view. Too unsettled to do much herself in the way of painting, Laraine gave most of her attention to instructing Moira. She pondered on doing so what a remarkable stroke of fate had brought them together. Normally she would never have met Moira, and if she had the girl was hardly the kind that she would have wanted for a friend. She was too demanding, too spoiled. Yet looking at her now and seeing how white and delicate her skin was, the hollowness of her cheekbones, the jerky movements as though all the nerves in her body were tightly stretched, Laraine felt very sorry for her; and eager to give her the kind of comfort and reassurance that she needed. She was careful to use an approach which not only made Moira feel alive but often on the edge of laughter. Unfortunately these happy moods never lasted long with Moira, and she soon lost interest in what she was doing.

'I'm not like you, Laraine,' she said after a burst of temper when she had thrown down her paintbrush. 'You're one of those people who delight in helping others. You have the patience to take your turn and share things with others. It's easy for you because you're healthy and full of good kind thoughts. Nothing has happened to shake them. But be careful, something might, and I'd like to see you then. I bet you'd become a taker like me.'

'I've noticed you're a taker,' Laraine said calmly. 'Nothing wrong with that if you give as well. And you're talking a lot of rubbish about me.'

She picked up the paintbrush and started to pack up the things.

'We'll go back to the car for a picnic tea. What about driving down to the sea to eat it?'

She looked at Moira's pale dispirited face, the nervous hand with which she smoothed back the bright hair, then picked up the painting equipment to take to the station wagon. When she returned Moira began talking again as if they had never left off.

'I'm a marauder and I don't mind confessing to it. That's why Charles and I understand each other. We don't have to say anything because we're two of a kind. He makes no appeal to my better nature—not that I have a better nature. Charles has an inflexible will. Do you know that? It's stimulating just fighting him.'

'He probably finds it stimulating too,' Laraine answered as she pushed the wheelchair towards the road.

'I wouldn't say that. One never knows what Charles is thinking and he always gets his own way in a tantalising, mocking manner which infuriates me. He's so nonchalant about it—the perfect gentleman on the surface with the iron hand underneath. What do you think about Charles?'

For a moment Laraine was taken aback, and thankful that Moira could not see her face. Otherwise she might have seen the telltale colour rushing to her face. Her hands tightened on the wheelchair.

'To begin with,' she said, 'I haven't known him long enough to form an opinion. I'd say you're fortunate to have such good friends around you, it certainly makes things easier for you.'

'Nothing and nobody can make things easier for me,' Moira snapped. 'I wish I were dead.'

To Laraine's dismay she burst into tears, and she reacted in the only way she knew by pushing her quickly to the station wagon on the road.

'Hi there!'

Rob's deep voice came towards them on the faint breeze,

lifting the cloud of depression that had descended.

Mindful of hiding Moira's distressed condition from his gaze, Laraine turned to greet him so that he stood immediately behind the wheelchair.

He was wearing riding clothes and carried a shotgun. Laraine eyed it with some apprehension. She hated guns.

'Just the person we wanted to see,' she cried lightheartedly. 'We're about to go down to the beach to eat our tea, and I was just hoping that a big stalwart young man like yourself would come along and carry Moira on to the sands. We might even give you some tea.'

Rob grinned. 'Done,' he answered. 'I'll put my gun in the back.'

Coolly Laraine said, 'You can take it in the front with you and drive. I'm going to sit in the back with Moira.'

Moira had been surreptitiously wiping her eyes and now Laraine turned swiftly to run the chair up the ramp and into the back. The back had been closed and they were on their way when Moira said stiffly,

'I'm sorry for making a scene.'

Laraine, seated along the side of the station wagon, leaned forward to push the bright hair from Moira's troubled eyes.

'Not to worry,' she said consolingly. 'It does a person good to give vent to their feelings. Better than bottling it up. You don't mind Rob coming with us, do you? I thought you'd enjoy it better on the sands. We can make a back rest for you with the picnic basket and some cushions.'

Moira shook her head and blew her nose into a wisp of a handkerchief.

They left the station wagon by the sand dunes and Rob swung Moira up easily into his arms while Laraine picked up the picnic basket, rugs and cushions. The sun was turning the beach into a carpet of gold warm and soft beneath their feet.

Laraine spread a cloth and put out the tea, Scotch pancakes which she decorated with golden curls of butter,

scones, minute sandwiches of meats and salad, Scotch eggs
and fruit with a carton of cream. She placed the empty
basket behind Moira and padded it with cushions, and
passed around plates. It was a jolly tea with Rob at his
audacious best. He teased them both in turn and ate his
share of the food.

Moira seemed to gain her former good humour. She
smiled with unusual amiability on Rob, who never guessed
he had interrupted her outburst of tears. Laraine had placed
everything with Moira in the centre so that sometimes she
found herself gazing across at Rob's profile against the
shimmering background of sea and sky. There was certainly
nothing anaemic or weak about it. He was really good-
looking and could charm when he chose.

One thing seemed sure—whatever might be the result of
Moira's plight, it was all over between her and Rob. Losing
his money was the best thing that could have happened to
him. Losing Moira—well, she was not so sure. Yet he had
stayed on because someone had to pick up the pieces when
Moira had been broken, though how precious those pieces
were to him there was no way of knowing. But she did
notice his hand stray across to take hold of Moira's in a
reassuring squeeze. The glint of the sun on his wristwatch
had caught Laraine's eye before she had looked away again
with a feeling of having trespassed on something personal.

On the way back Rob put Moira beside him on the driving seat with Laraine squeezing in on her other side. When
she began to hum the first bars of *Loch Lomond* Rob
soon joined in with a pleasant baritone. Then Moira joined
in too. They were all singing lustily on arriving at Lochdoone, and when George came out to see what all the noise
was about, his face became creased into a smile as he saw
his daughter looking so happy.

To Laraine it was a happy ending to what at first had
promised to be a disappointing afternoon. Dared she hope
that the evening would be as successful? Accompanying
Moira in the lift on their way upstairs she wondered why all

had been pleasant, until she remembered that Charles was coming that evening.

'What shall I wear this evening?'

Moira wheeled the chair to the spacious wardrobes and flung open doors to reveal dozens of dresses. Laraine watched as she impatiently pushed one dress after another aside on its hanger, beautiful dresses which must have cost a lot of money. Then she smiled approvingly as Moira's beautifully manicured fingers touched a tartan evening skirt.

'That, I think, with the lovely white silk blouse and the matching tartan stole,' she said warmly. 'Now I'm going to help you on to the bed to rest until Mrs Dougal comes to help you to dress.'

After massaging her neck, Laraine left Moira lying on her bed with pads of witch hazel on her eyes and went to her own room. There was plenty of time to dress for the evening, so she relaxed luxuriously in a perfumed bath, then towelled herself vigorously after stepping from under the cold shower. The afternoon spent on the beach in the sun had given her skin the warm glow of a peach and her eyes looked clear and bright. Her dress was nothing spectacular, just a glazed cotton with a round flattering neckline and pretty design of tiny roses on a white background. A white beaded necklace and matching studs in her ears threw into relief the widely spaced eyes and the sweet serenity of her expression. Her hair, newly washed, was flicked into place and curled softly around her slender neck and face.

As she dressed Laraine wondered about Charles McGreyfarne. She supposed that by now, on different ground, she should be able to greet him quite impersonally. For some reason he appeared to have a deepseated unwillingness to cross the barrier between them of being strangers. Maybe she was just as unwilling herself to do so. Common sense told her that it was right. After all, he belonged to Moira. That was something she could not forget, she reflected, as she left her room to go to see if Moira was ready.

She was, looking lovely in the tartan skirt and white silk blouse. Her golden hair formed an aura around her face, and she looked less pale. The beauty box was open on the dressing table, Mrs Dougal had gone and Moira was applying blue eye-shadow to her eyelids.

'How do I look?' she asked anxiously as she returned the eye-shadow to the box. 'I want to look my best for Charles. He's known so many beautiful women.'

'So what?' Laraine said reassuringly. 'He's chosen you, and you look very sweet.'

'Not as sweet as you.' At Laraine's startled gaze, she went on hastily, 'You walked into the room just now looking so fresh and glowing with your hair swinging softly about your face. I can't do that. I want to run to Charles and feel his arms close around me to lift me off my feet. I can't bear what this is doing to me and to him.'

Her eyes were filled with anguish and all reserve, all petulance had dropped away.

'What is it doing to him?' Laraine asked quietly. 'You told me yourself that he accepted you as you are.'

'He did—he does—I mean——' Moira stopped and lowered her eyes, fingering the tartan stole while refusing to meet Laraine's steady gaze. 'He's different these last few weeks, in some way he's different from what he was before you came. Do you know what I mean?'

'No, I don't.'

'I don't mean that he's less kind or anything like that. He seems to be so far away at times.' Her hands moved restlessly to pluck the fringe of the stole. 'He's not said anything to you about me, has he?'

Laraine's laugh was a little mocking. 'My dear girl, it takes your Charles all his time to be polite to me! I can only put it down to the fact that he regards my being here as something like a threat to your ever walking again. Quite naturally he sees you now as quite happy to be fussed over by everyone, himself included.'

Moira nodded. 'Charles is no fool. He probably knows

me better than I do myself. I'm greedy and very possessive. I want Charles, Daddy and Rob.'

Laraine said carefully, 'It's really quite simple. Ask yourself which man you love the best. Naturally the love you feel for your father is vastly different from the love you have for the man in your life.'

Moira pouted. 'I know that. I happen to want all of them. I know it's silly, but that's how I am.'

Laraine said gently, 'In the circumstances it isn't surprising. A wheelchair isn't the best place to help sort things out.'

But Moira was not listening. She hastily propelled herself to the dressing table where she took a cigarette from a box and lighted it. Inhaling the smoke, she expelled it again with an air of command.

'Tell Charles to come up when he arrives to carry me down to dinner.'

'I will with pleasure if you'll put that cigarette out. You can hardly go down in his arms with your breath reeking of tobacco. It's enough to put any man off.'

To her dismay Laraine felt a tremor in her voice and she opened the door with a hand that was not quite steady and left the room.

CHAPTER SEVEN

DINNER had reached the coffee stage beside a log fire in the lounge. Good food, good conversation, and warm hospitality had created an atmosphere of good will that lingered on after they had left the dining room. There was still light coming from the tall windows and the flame-licked logs crackled bright, warm and golden.

Charles had carried Moira down to dinner and later into the lounge for coffee where she now sat between him and Rob to face Laraine, Margaret and George across the hearth. Margaret, Laraine thought, looked very sweet in pale blue and her gaze had lingered tenderly on Moira, who had been the centre of the gathering all evening.

But it was Charles who dominated the scene for Laraine. He combined compassion and chivalry with a kind of arrogance that was wholly charming. His compassion for Moira gave the impression that he felt in some way responsible for the blow fate had dealt her. He might even misconstrue her refusal to see yet another specialist, taking it as a woman's natural abhorrence at being examined by another male, and perhaps a kind of fear of further disappointment. But would he be satisfied with an invalid wife? Was he so cynical as to have chosen with head and heart in that order?

Laraine quivered with the knowledge that he was too virile, too much a man to forgo the generosity of passion, the prodigality of love. But if Charles puzzled her it was a relief to find that the evening had not been the ordeal she had expected. Everything had gone smoothly, rather like a family gathering with no wrong note anywhere.

While coffee was being served George handed around cigarettes. Laraine and Margaret refused, and Moira, reaching out to take one by force of habit, suddenly surprised everyone by withdrawing her hand. Her eyes met Laraine's and they both smiled.

George, Rob and Charles had cheroots with the latter bending forward to accept a light from George. Straightening indolently, Charles blew out a line of smoke ceilingwards, then directed a narrow-eyed gaze at Moira.

'What's the joke?' he asked as he leaned back against the fireplace.

Moira shrugged. 'Laraine is reforming me,' she admitted. 'I've been smoking too much anyway.'

Rob's voice held a hint of satire. 'Laraine's influence must be pretty potent. I've never known you to give anything up voluntarily.'

Moira's look at him was withering. 'Just because you gave up drinking you needn't think you're unique!'

'I didn't give up drinking. I couldn't afford it. And it wasn't the only thing I gave up either.' Rob looked at his wrist watch in the manner of someone thoroughly fed up with himself. 'Which reminds me, I have work to do before bed.'

He drank his coffee, lifted the hand with the cheroot between his fingers and wished them farewell. For the rest of the evening they talked, what about Laraine could never have remembered. Then Charles was picking Moira up in his arms to take her to her room. Laraine opened the door for them and strolled out across the hall and out of the front door, presumbly to leave Margaret and George together.

Bright crimson streaks painted the sky as a sliver of moon arose—too early to go to bed since she had to wait for Margaret to say her goodnight to Moira in her room before she went to give her the nightly massage. Laraine hugged her arms across her chest. Her mind was a confusion these days.

It was all very difficult to clarify her ideas. I've been very silly, she told herself. All that wonderful dream for helping Moira had really come to nothing. A great unhappiness seized her at the thought of never seeing Charles again. The last scene with Harvey had somehow soured London for her. She seemed to be held in a vacuum from which there was no escape because she was hemmed in by her love for Charles. Perhaps it was not meant for her to know love, peace and happiness. Certainly it was taking her a long time to find it—and without Charles it was impossible.

She shivered, for the air had a bite in it, and turned to go indoors. The last thing she wanted was for Charles to come out and find her there. There was no sign of him in the hall and her steps slowed as she entered the lounge. George and Margaret were talking companionably where she had left them.

George was saying, 'It's no use, Margaret. I've made up my mind to take Moira to Rome whether she likes it or not. She doesn't know yet.'

'Should you?' Margaret looked concerned. 'Even if it's against her wishes?'

She looked up as Laraine approached and patted the empty place beside her on the roomy sofa. George gave her a welcome smile and she sat down as he answered.

'The thing has to be done,' he said firmly. 'It won't be necessary to tell her in advance. I shall make all arrangements. The specialist in Rome is going on holiday and has promised to see her when he returns home. When the time comes I'm hoping she'll have the good sense to go.'

'I see,' said Margaret thoughtfully. 'You don't think you ought to take her on a holiday first—say a cruise—to prepare her for it?'

George leaned forward to crush out the butt of his cheroot, using an ashtray from a low table nearby. Then he straightened and looked with some exasperation at Margaret sitting beside him.

'What's wrong with Moira that she needs to recuperate before having an examination?' he scoffed. 'The girl isn't going in for a serious examination, we're just seeking another opinion. Dash it all, something has to be done before her muscles begin to deteriorate from lack of exercise.'

His voice was mocking with one eyebrow lifted in faint amusement as he looked past Margaret to Laraine. She was listening with wide-eyed interest and he intercepted her gaze frankly.

'What do you say, Laraine? Would you say that my daughter is in good shape?'

She accepted his challenge with a smile and a slight deepening of her colour. His refusal to be denied a second opinion had won her respect. The poor man was aware, no doubt, that he spoiled his daughter terribly and that Margaret did too. It was easy to see that Moira would go on playing them up without someone to jolly her along into positive action, and that was what she was here for. But could she go against Margaret, whom she also liked and respected?

'It's hardly for me to say,' she began hesitantly.

'To say what?'

Charles had entered the room and was walking across the carpet with his long economical stride. Margaret rose as she saw him, and said with a smile, 'I'll go up to say goodnight to Moira and leave you all to it.'

She passed Charles, who stood there with his hands thrust into his pockets, eyebrows raised.

George said, 'Take a seat, Charles. We're discussing my very stubborn daughter. Well, Laraine? I asked you a question.'

She found it more bearable to avoid the intent look that Charles bestowed upon her.

'I agree with you,' she said. 'The sooner Moira sees this specialist the better. I can't see her ever being in good health confined as she is to a wheelchair. I also think it's a good idea to arrange everything in advance as you propose to do.'

George answered with undisguised fervour, 'I knew you'd agree. You've been so good for Moira since you came. You don't know how grateful I am for what you've done.'

Slow colour stained her cheeks, her throat. 'Oh ... I haven't done much,' she answered with painful hesitation. 'In fact I doubt whether my visit has done much if anything for Moira.'

'You mean you aren't happy here?'

'Dear me, no! I would have been happier if I could have done more.' There was pain in her voice at the tiredness of his eyes as hope seemed to leave them. 'That doesn't mean that I think there's no hope of Moira walking again, and ... and you mustn't worry.'

'Well, well,' drawled Charles. He was standing relaxed and mocking with the fireplace behind his wide shoulders. 'I'm sure I can't improve on that, no matter how I try.'

Laraine looked up and knew a flash of exquisite, unhappy contact as he met her eyes with derision in his own.

George laughed and eased a tension that was almost tangible.

'I'm more than lucky to have such friends,' he exclaimed. 'And if I didn't know you better I'd swear you sounded a trifle cynical.'

'I'm sure Laraine thinks so,' Charles replied suavely.

Her throat felt constricted, but she forced herself to speak. 'What I think is irrelevant. But then I'm sure that won't worry you.'

'You'd be surprised. I can be quite sensitive when I want to be. Ask George.'

George laughed. 'Stop teasing the girl, Charles. What do you think of the idea of taking Moira to Rome later and not giving her time to refuse?'

'I'm in favour of her going. You're far too lenient with your daughter, George. Now if she was mine ...'

'I know—you'd take her by the hair of her head. Well, I might have to do just that.' George chuckled. 'Don't take any notice of me, Laraine. I only wish I had some of Charles in me. I'd do as I thought fit and be hanged to what people said or thought. Maybe one day I will.'

He leaned sideways to pat Laraine's hand, smiling down

at her across the space Margaret had left between them on the sofa. But the smile did not reach his eyes as he let out an unhappy sigh.

'It's difficult to decide what to do for the best sometimes. Anyway, I'm glad you're here. I'm going to rely upon your help during the next few weeks.' He turned to address Charles, who was looking down at him with a closed expression, and added, 'I'll fetch that book I promised you. I left it in the library.'

His sudden departure from the room put Laraine in a quandary. She could hardly go upstairs until Margaret had left Moira without Charles coming to the conclusion that she was running away from him. It would never do to let him suspect even that his presence upset her. So she sat tight, uncomfortably aware of a tension that seemed to stretch across her nerves. It was impossible for her to look up at him as he leaned back nonchalantly against the fireplace.

'You really do suffer for other folks, don't you?' he said sardonically. 'Or is it an act?'

His last words really needled her so much so that she lifted wide indignant eyes to his narrow-eyed gaze.

'What do you mean?'

A faint smile showed in his eyes. 'Only that it's so rare these days to find someone like you who really cares for her fellow men. It's a breed that seems to be dying out. How interesting it's going to be to see just how far you're prepared to go with all this caring.'

'I don't know what you mean.'

'Putting it rather crudely, woman stuff. If you continue to look at George the way you looked at him just now before he left the room there's no knowing where it can lead you.'

Laraine drew in a deep breath and found herself glaring at him with more fury than she had thought herself capable of. Clenching her hands, she let him have the full blast of her wrath.

'How dare you talk to me like that? You forget that not

only am I not your employee but I am also not your guest
any longer. It's none of your business what I do!'

He said mildly, 'I don't agree. Here you are, admitted
into a close circle of friends which you can tear apart with
one innocent look from those long-lashed eyes, and you
expect me to stand mutely by while you do so.'

Laraine fought hard to hold her temper in check because
it was only by so doing that she could hope to get her point
across. While she was bewildered at the way he regarded her
as some femme fatale, she knew that his good opinion mattered to her. Frankly, this last thought increased her bewilderment, since he was conceited, egotistical and insult-
ing. On the other hand, there were qualities in him that
were worthy of respect. At the moment she was too upset to
pinpoint them. What mattered was that they were there.

Her laugh was brittle. 'I've never heard such nonsense!'
she exclaimed. 'What on earth can I do to upset this ... this
close circle you talk about? Since you're so concerned about
it why don't you make it impregnable by marrying Moira?'

She was unprepared for the sudden gleam of anger in his
eyes which he glossed over with a trace of mockery so
quickly that she wondered if it had really been there.

'Dear, dear,' he drawled, and she wondered why his voice
had to be so disturbingly deep and musical instead of
grating on the eardrums. 'You are in a hurry to get me
married! That's the second time you've suggested it.' His
lips twisted a little to show white teeth fleetingly, cruelly.
'I'm no boy to be satisfied with someone who hasn't fully
matured. I've waited a long time for a suitable partner and
I can wait a little longer.'

Laraine was aghast. 'You talk like someone considering a
business arrangement! Is that all marriage means to you? I
can't believe that ... that anyone could be so ... so philo-
sophical about the most important thing in life. Haven't
you ever been in love?'

He raised a brow in the infuriating way he had and
asked mockingly,

'Have you?'

Laraine ignored the dragging pain at her heart. Afterwards she supposed it would have been wiser to cut short the incident and leave the room instead of staring blindly up at him. It occurred to her then why he had been so antagonistic towards her. To him she was a second Moira, the unawakened type who bored him. She was also young and healthy, sound in wind and limb, and Moira was not. Therefore any temptation her presence might hold for him was related to the angry, bitter desire he had to hurt her. Furthermore, the knowledge that she was not the kind of woman he would choose to marry only made her feel very young and vulnerable and hurt her deeply.

Beneath the morass of mixed emotions, anger, a sense of humiliation, was the desire to go right away from any further hurt he might inflict upon her. It was no use wishing for George to reappear to help her end the unwelcome conversation. Then Charles was speaking again.

'Evidently you haven't been in love,' he said.

'I can understand how you feel,' she answered evasively.

'Do you?' He strolled towards her noiselessly over the carpet after a kind of lunge from where he had been standing. 'Tell me, how in the world can you even begin to understand the desires and frustrations of a healthy virile man? Most of you city dwellers have emotions that skim lightly over the surface. You haven't the time for the finer instincts. They lie too far beneath the surface for you to take the time to drag them out into the open.'

He had by now come too close to her for comfort, and she stood up in a state of panic. 'For someone who lives so far away from city dwellers you know an awful lot about them. If some girl some time let you down don't take it out on me,' she said with hands clenched. 'Now, if you'll excuse me . . .'

Before she could move he had swept her into his arms to imprison her quivering mouth beneath his own. His lips were firm, ruthless and demanding, and Laraine felt them with a sense of shock culminating into a sudden delight. Her blood raced madly through her veins and her whole being sprang into life. By sheer masculine brute strength he had opened up a new world which she never knew existed and for moments she was shattered by the underlying wonder of it. She was blind to everything until the thought that he had come to her from Moira broke through.

To descend from such emotional heights and behave normally would have been too much to ask even from someone more experienced. Yet Laraine achieved it with a show of calm dignity although her heart threatened to knock a hole in her ribs.

Pitting all her strength against him, she felt his arms slacken and, once free, she looked up at him witheringly.

'I hardly think I deserved that,' she said with scorn. Then she turned and fled from the room.

Much later that evening after giving herself time to calm down before going in to see Moira and returning to her room, Laraine lay wide-eyed and very far from sleep in her bed. It seemed to her that a whole lifetime had passed since she had left Harvey to begin a new chapter in her life. Their association had held no passion. She had known where she had been with him. There had been no uncertainties, no feeling of panic.

While she had known that her feelings for Harvey could never have been anything resembling love there had been a kind of companionship between them. Life with Harvey had been like sharing a punt on a quiet lake. The emotion she now knew as love was not a bit like that. It was a raging, relentless current that swept her along frighteningly against her will. What happened to her in Charles' arms was altogether beyond reason. But it had happened, and life would never be the same again.

CHAPTER EIGHT

In the days that followed, Laraine found her job a little more rewarding. Moira was, at last, showing more life, more interest in things around her. Most mornings they went out, weather permitting, with their painting gear. Laraine was inspired by the scenery, the ever-changing colours and growth around her was absorbed absolutely by her artistic senses. She loved the delicate new leafage of the beech, the old pines resplendent in sun and shade and the majesty of the sturdy oaks spreading out their branches in regal splendour. They just begged to be put on canvas along with the lochs, the glens and the rainbow-coloured hills.

After living for so long in a traffic-ridden city Laraine felt her heart go out to the mellowed beauty of a country that had lain unspoiled for centuries. There were moments when she sat beside Moira, lost in her own private ecstasy. But not for long. With little interest in her own abortive attempts at being an artist, Moira was forever demanding attention.

Laraine's company, her nearness, the generous warmth of her young vitality had charmed away to a certain degree the stealthy shadow of paralysed limbs that was forever with her. But unlike Laraine, she was incapable of losing herself in the splendour of fabulous colour which saturated the earth and sky around her.

Laraine gave her every attention with unstinting warmth, understanding in her compassion the consuming restlessness aggravated by her paralysis. She knew that her father had been right to engage a companion for her instead of a nurse who would remind her constantly of her disability. Most of the day he was engaged with matters on the estate with Rob, but he gave the rest of his time to Moira. Unfortunately his precocious daughter seemed to take a delight in turning his suggestions down. Even the building of a swimming pool in the grounds failed to arouse her enthusiasm. The scheme was already well under way when he had suggested them going to take a look at it.

There had been a little scene after breakfast that morning when Moira had refused ungraciously. For embarrassed moments Laraine had stood there to witness Moira venting her wrath on her father. They were in the hall, having left the dining room. Moira was in her wheelchair and George was on his way to his study.

'What's the use of the pool anyway?' she had snapped at him with a hint of malicious anger in her voice. 'A swimming pool isn't going to do me any good when I can't use my legs. Why don't you stop kidding yourself?'

For a moment George had paled, then he had turned on his heel to answer a telephone call in his study. It was then that Laraine looked down on her charge with an unbearable urge to shake her.

'That wasn't very kind, was it?' she asked quietly.

'I don't feel kind. I wish everybody would leave me alone.'

'If they did you'd jolly well soon be moaning. That's one of the things I dislike about you, Moira—you're too full of your own cocoon of self-pity. Another thing I don't like about you is your malicious desire to hurt others and to go on hurting.'

Moira was furious. 'That isn't true! How dare you criticise me? What do you know about being trapped in a wheelchair?'

'That's true, I know nothing of being a helpless invalid. But you're certainly nothing of the kind,' Laraine told her gently. 'You don't have to be in that wheelchair. It's up to you, like I said before.'

'Oh, go away!' Moira cried. 'You'll have me doing good works next for those worse off than myself ... Worse off than myself ... that's a laugh, isn't it?'

Moira was now verging on the brink of hysterics when Charles suddenly strode in through the open front door. Dramatically, she held out her arms towards him.

'Oh, Charles!' she cried. 'Take me away—I want to die!'

'What is this?' he queried, sharing a narrow-eyed gaze between the two of them. 'Glad you're waiting for me. We shall have to step on it, or we shall be late.'

Moira had leaned forward to seize one of his hands as he had approached and she now hung on to it to stare up at him open-mouthed.

'Be late for what?' she demanded, her anger momentarily forgotten.

'Why, this is Wednesday, your usual day for visiting the hospital for treatment. Don't say you've forgotten?'

'Oh, no!' Her face puckered in distress. 'I won't go.'

'Oh yes, you will.' Without more ado Charles swept her up into his arms and carried her out to his car. He had scarcely looked at Laraine and he was murmuring words of comfort as he went.

'Was that Charles?'

She turned as George came from his study, and nodded. He was smiling.

'One word from Charles and she does exactly what he tells her. I can see I'm using the wrong techniques. Like to see the pool? They're going to tile it.'

'I'd love to,' said Laraine, who was still seeing the swift softening of Charles' ruthless, handsome face bent over Moira.

At the light touch of George's hand on her arm as they went outdoors, she noticed the sudden mask of weariness on his face. It was a terrible position for him to be in if, as she thought, his daughter's accident was in the way of happiness with the woman he loved—Margaret. And there was Charles too, who was just aching for Moira to recover. Also there was Rob, who was staying on because of his compassion for the girl. Come to think of it, Moira was responsible for shaping four lives—her own as well.

It was a lovely morning with the grounds dreaming in the sunshine. There were four men working at the pool in a sheltered spot at the back of the house and they greeted George with the familiarity and respect that a nice man like him usually receives. Laraine found herself looking upon the pool for the first time, sheltered by trees on three sides which included the house. The open side had a southern aspect and would be gloriously warm in the summer. Right now the sun burned down and the men were working stripped to the waist and displaying well-muscled torsoes. The oldest of them could not have been forty and they looked at Laraine in frank admiration.

She gave them a warm smile in return, then turned to speak to George before they noticed her embarrassment.

'Moira is going to love this when it's finished,' she vouchsafed. 'Could she swim before . . .'

'Yes. I can too. Can you?'

Laraine nodded. 'One good thing is that she won't be afraid of the water. It's a good idea for you to have the pool.'

He brightened and she felt compassion for him. He was probably losing touch with some of his friends since his daughter's accident, because she must have proved a full-time job. What parties they had at Lochdoone now were given with Moira in mind, so it had not been easy for him.

With this in mind Laraine went on, 'Anything that will take Moira's thoughts from herself and her condition is a good thing. The trouble is that she might be still suffering from the shock of finding herself in a wheelchair. Also she could be suffering from a deep sense of injustice that it's happened to her.'

George agreed. 'You could be right, but I'm adamant about her going to Rome in the near future. Thanks for reassuring me. It's comforting to have someone around who understands.'

He went on to tell her about the swimming pool, taking her to where the tiles were stacked to show her the patterns involved. It was some time before they retraced their steps to the house to meet Rob halfway. There was something he wanted to discuss with George and they walked back together. Laraine was in between them and George had a careless arm around her slender shoulders. He was looking lighthearted and dropped a joke at which they were all laughing when they saw Charles. Apparently he had returned from the hospital having left Moira there and had come in search of them. He looked high, wide and arrogantly self-assured. But there was no tenderness in his eyes as they rested for moments on her laughing expression before noting George's arm around her shoulders.

'I've come at Margaret's request to borrow Laraine,' he said smoothly. 'Since Moira won't be returning until lunch I take it that you can spare her.'

'Of course. I'm afraid we're very selfish,' George admitted in such a lighthearted way that Charles lifted a brow. 'We've never even discussed her having time off, and we should have done.'

'That's all right,' said Laraine. 'Am I to go now, then?'

'So long,' said Charles, taking her arm. 'See you later.'

Crossly she thought, he hasn't given George time to say anything more—really, he takes too much on himself! But Charles did not appear to have such thoughts as he took her to his car and opened the door to the front seat. He had put on speed and they had left Lochdoone before she spoke.

'You looked quite happy when I arrived just now. What was the joke?'

'Joke?' she turned wide clear eyes at his profile. 'Nothing much. It was good to see George in a joking mood.'

Dryly he said, 'I'm sure it was. More than one could say of Moira when I arrived. She said you'd been bullying her.'

Laraine was taken aback. 'Did she? I wonder why?'

'It isn't true, then?'

A stubborn streak in her stiffened a resolve not to tell him. Instead, she said, 'You've known her longer than I have. You should know.'

'You mean you aren't telling me about it?'

'That's right.'

He gave her a swift sharp glance. 'I understood that you were here to help Moira, not her father,' he said curtly.

'Her father is in it too,' she replied coolly. 'I'd guarantee that he's suffered in his way as much as Moira has. Rob is concerned as well.'

'Sure they're concerned. We all are, only don't give everything you have in consoling them. They were over the worst when you arrived.'

Laraine stiffened beside him. 'That's a callous thing to say!' she snapped. 'But then you're only acting in character as usual.'

'So are you. You can't be all things to all people, my child. One has to draw the line, especially in your case.'

'Why in my case?'

'Because you feel things too deeply. It doesn't do much good, you know. Much better to do things normally instead of going off at the deep end and achieving little.'

'If that's your maxim I don't see much result on your part.' His profile, outlined against the inside of the car, the line of his lean firm jaw, the bright hair—all combined to put her off her stride. 'And I wish you'd stop regarding me as a femme fatale!'

'Then you shouldn't give me cause. I'd say for a newcomer you were doing very well when I arrived just now.'

She gave him a long furious stare. If he thought that he was going to get the better of her this time he would not succeed. She would show him!

'Really? At least they've behaved themselves, which is more than I can say of you, with a comparative newcomer,' she retorted.

His ironic gaze slid sideways upon her with an expression she could not read—it filled her with discomfort. 'You mean the kiss? You asked for that.' He grinned mockingly at her rising colour. 'There was nothing in it except the urge to shake you out of that little dream world of yours.'

He had spoken disdainfully, rejecting explanation, and in

that moment she hated him. The feeling gave her courage.

'I know that,' she replied coolly. 'But it went to show how much I've shaken you out of your dream world too.'

He made no answer for several moments as he slowed up to drive around a combine harvester. Laraine noticed angrily that he appeared serene and she longed to shake him. If he had gone all out to shake her he had succeeded, but not for all the world would she tell him so.

'My dear child, your presence here has done little more than irritate me from the day you arrived. I only wish it had achieved the same effect on George and Rob,' he told her carelessly.

Laraine gave up. She said no more. It was easy to see that seeing her on such excellent terms with George and Rob had made him angry. It was clear that Charles did not welcome her into life either at McGreyfarne or Lochdoone, and she had to accept it. She swallowed on a hurt deep inside her. The world that Charles moved in was far different from her own. His was a world of wild Border country where old beliefs still existed from ancestors which made her own look pale in comparison—like the horsemen she had seen when first Charles had driven her from the station on the day of her arrival. They had carried the stamp of a fierce proud race, and Charles was no exception.

The combine harvester was the only vehicle they passed, apart from a postman on a bike to whom Charles lifted a careless hand in greeting. Two weatherbeaten old cronies seated beneath the spread of a massive oak in the tiny village had also acknowledged his salute when they passed.

He drove swiftly and confidently with firm brown hands, using the car wheel in a deceptively light hold. Then came the crunch of gravel as he swung the car off the road and on to the drive. The morning sun reflecting blindingly on McGreyfarne greeted them as they pulled up silently at the massive front door. Laraine was conscious of sweet scents coming from the gardens, underlain with a tang of sea air mixed with pine, not all sweetness.

In order to avoid any assistance from Charles she was out of the car in a trice and going lightly up the steps to the open front door. He might not have been with her for all the notice she had taken of him. After all, what was he, an unaccountable friend or an enemy? Laraine moistened lips that felt dry and cool, then her embarrassment vanished at the sight of Mac.

Without warning he emerged from the shadows in the hall, bounding joyfully to greet her with a delighted leap ending with an endearing wuff! wuff! Taken unawares by his weight and exuberance, Laraine was knocked completely off her balance. She reeled backwards and it seemed inevitable that she would crash down the marble steps behind her, steps that moments before had been ascended so lightly.

For one agonizing moment her slender form was suspended in mid-air and the next found a solid wall behind her preventing her fall. Bands of steel were closing around her. Then an oath followed by a command to Mac was vibrating through her whole body from the powerful chest against which she was imprisoned.

Laraine had closed her eyes, fearing the worst, and she lay back against Charles thoroughly spent. The relief was so great that she felt near to tears. Her whole body was trembling and it was humiliating to know that he was aware of it.

He spoke softly from somewhere above her head into her hair.

'Easy now. Just relax and stand still for a moment leaning against me. That was some shock you had.'

Laraine tried to draw in a deep steadying breath, but her chest felt flat and the air trembled in her throat. For one thing she was sure that he was not aware of how tight he held her. For another it was impossible to relax in his embrace. She was too tense, and more than a little frightened, not only by her miraculous escape from serious injury but by Charles himself.

In those frightening moments it became suddenly clear that it was far better for them to continue their association on an impersonal note than to become too involved. She was not the bold type of girl who would rejoice in any kind of association with him. He was too arrogant, too demanding, too disturbing, too everything for her peace of mind. She must have been mad to allow any softening of her feelings towards him. Let him ride through his countryside, toss his cabers, and dance his reels, she wanted no part of him.

She opened her eyes, aware that Mac had retreated and was lying on all paws with his chin resting on his two front ones. Stronger than the desire to leave those suffocating arms was the thought of him punishing Mac.

'You ... you won't punish Mac, will you?' she said, loosening his grip by standing up straight and pushing back her elbows against him.

He released her slowly. 'Go to the kitchen, Mac,' he said quietly, and slid his hands down to her slender waist. 'Sure you're all right?'

When Laraine lifted her head to look up at him he had moved to her side while retaining one arm around her.

'Yes, thanks,' she answered. 'About Mac ...'

He said curtly, 'I'm not an ogre. I'm quite as capable of loving a dog as you are.' His arm dropped abruptly and she was free. Or was she? She had the feeling that she would never feel free again as he spoke again. 'Come into the library and have a drink to steady your nerves.'

'No, thank you.' Her voice sounded tremulous, to her disgust. 'I don't need one, and I don't want to upset your aunt. There's no need to do so. It was nothing really, since you saved me from a very nasty accident. I want to thank you.'

'There's nothing to thank me for,' he replied sardonically. 'Mac sent you flying back into my arms. I find it remarkable that he should be so fond of you, because he's always been a one-man dog.'

Laraine was looking up at him, at the bright hair, the lean face that had an expression of bitter humour, and she wondered why. Beneath his intent regard her colour rose in her cheeks.

Mockingly he said, 'Your colour is coming back.'

It was then that she noticed the pale look around his nostrils, as if he too had received a shock of some kind. Or could it be a trick of the light? After the brightness of outdoors the sudden dimness in the hall could be misleading. That was it, of course. Nothing could disturb the calm of Charles McGreyfarne. If there was one thing one could be sure about it was that.

Laraine gave a breathy small laugh and hoped it sounded convincing.

'That's comforting,' she said lightly. 'Do I look normal enough not to arouse any attention from your aunt when I see her?'

It was a mistake to invite his perusal of her face which now deepened into a rosy glow, showing the clear healthy whites of her eyes, her rosy mouth and small pearly teeth. A gleam came into his eyes, to go again before she could say what it was. Then he was staring beyond her towards the staircase, and the softening of his features into a look of tenderness smote her heart.

'You'll soon find out,' he said. 'Here's Aunt Margaret now.'

Margaret came towards them eagerly across the hall. She was wearing a cashmere suit in a soft grey and she looked serene and untroubled.

'Thank you for coming, Laraine,' she exclaimed, kissing her on the cheek. 'It was important for me to see you without Moira being present. I'll explain as we go upstairs.' To Charles, 'See you at lunch.'

They went upstairs arm in arm as Charles strode away from them across the hall.

'About Moira,' Margaret began. 'Since her accident she has flatly refused to buy any dresses or anything. It's under-

standable really, since she would have to go in the wheelchair. Also clothes don't mean the same to her now, poor
dear. So I had this idea of making her an evening dress,
though really it's a skirt and blouse.'

'How nice,' Laraine said warmly. 'Can you sew, then?'

Margaret nodded. 'I had a friend once years ago who
worked for a famous fashion house in London and she
taught me a lot of the tricks of the trade. They've come in
very useful.'

'I'm sure,' agreed Laraine. 'And where do I come in?'

Margaret hesitated long enough to open a door along the
corridor at the head of the stairs to usher her in. They
entered a sitting room with a model of a bust and torso in
one corner and a sewing machine, along with other comfortable furniture.

'My workroom,' she said modestly. 'I hope you don't
mind if I use you to model the evening dress and blouse
I've made for Moira. You're about the same size, willowy
and small-waisted.'

'Not at all,' Laraine replied warmly. 'It's gorgeous.'

She looked with delight at a luscious shimmering long
skirt in panne velvet along with the sheer luxury of an ultra-
feminine matching blouse in georgette. The pattern of the
print was the same for both garments. Roses of a delicate
pink were printed on a background of blue and silver which
gave a shimmering effect of richness. The skirt needed a
waistband and the blouse was tacked together for Laraine
to try on.

'You like it?' Margaret asked anxiously. 'Do you think
Moira will?'

Laraine gave a sigh of admiration. 'She'll adore it,' she
smiled. 'How sweet of you to think of giving her such a
wonderful surprise.'

She beamed happily at Margaret, who was now looking
relieved.

'The trouble is,' Margaret said, 'I shall need you for
another fitting later in order to ensure a perfect fit. We shall

have to arrange it when Moira isn't around. I want it to be a complete surprise.'

'Of course,' Laraine agreed with a laugh of pure pleasure. 'You don't know how glad I am to be made use of. I've done so little up to now.'

'Nonsense.' Margaret slipped the blouse over Laraine's slim bare shoulders. 'I'm sure we're all glad that you've come. How is Moira's father?'

'He's fine. I think he'll feel better when Moira has been to Rome to see the specialist.'

There was a brief silence while Margaret adjusted the blouse before she answered. Laraine was curious as to why she had asked about George when they had met so recently at dinner less than a week previously. But she was determined not to show it.

'I'm sure we all will.' Margaret adjusted the blouse on one shoulder, then stepped back to see the result. 'I'd like to see Charles settled—and I'm sure he wants it too. It won't be the same if Moira never walks again, but I don't think he'll mind. He has his work cut out here on the estate and he will take good care of her.'

Laraine caught her breath for a moment in her throat. 'It won't be much of a marriage, will it?'

Margaret shrugged. 'It isn't exactly what I would want for Charles, but he'll cope. There, that will do, I think.'

She began to slip the blouse off Laraine's arms and carried it across to the model bust. The absorbed expression on her face as she fitted it to the model gave her a young, expressive sweetness. Laraine decided that Margaret McGreyfarne was not capable of a mean thought, and said impulsively,

'I'm surprised that you haven't married. You're so attractive, and nice—and I mean that.'

The older woman smiled rather sadly. 'Maybe it isn't meant for us all to marry. In any case, life is always changing. Do you not find it so?'

Laraine nodded. 'But not changing in the way we want.'

'In what way do you want it to change, Laraine? I suppose like every girl you want to marry and raise a family? I can hardly see you as a career girl. You aren't the type. Now, this Harvey you know—are you going back to him?'

Laraine wondered whether it was a leading question and decided to be wary. 'I'm not going back to anyone,' she answered firmly. 'Harvey was only a friend. You're right about wanting to marry. I want to some day, of course.'

'Any particular man in mind?'

'I hope to fall in love first.'

Margaret nodded. 'That's essential.' She laughed. 'I'm sure it won't be long before some nice man snatches you up. You're much too pretty and charming to remain single for long. I'd like to make your trousseau. I've already made Moira's, but she doesn't know it. The negligé only as yet.'

Laraine moistened dry lips. 'You're sure of her getting married quite soon, then?'

Margaret shrugged. 'Who knows? I suppose it's in the lap of the gods whether she'll walk again.'

'I think she will. She has to do for Charles' sake, doesn't she?'

Margaret did not answer. Instead she signalled Laraine to follow her to a chintz-covered chest serving as a seat. Inside was the kind of cobwebby negligé a girl dreams about, frothy silk and lace with ribbons, all delicately made.

Laraine breathed in the delicate scent of pot-pourri as the garments were revealed between layers of tissue paper.

'They're gorgeous!' she cried. 'Thanks for showing them to me.'

Margaret replaced each garment almost reverently. 'I think every girl should have beautiful things to wear on her honeymoon. A pity that girls today don't seem to think much beyond a nightdress, and not always that. They miss such a lot by not being so essentially feminine.'

'I'll bear that in mind,' Laraine promised lightheartedly. 'I've always had pretty underclothes, though. They cost the earth these days.'

'Then let's hope you marry someone who can afford

them. But I'm sure the financial end won't bother you.'

'No, it won't,' Laraine replied as Morag entered with mid-morning coffee and biscuits.

The morning went swiftly and all too soon they were going down to lunch. It had been arranged for Charles to return to McGreyfarne with Moira for them to all have lunch together. They arrived downstairs to find Moira and Charles already in the dining room. Charles was looking down at Moira, whom he had placed in an easy chair near the tall sunlit windows. His white smile did much to relieve the taut line of his jaw, so familiar to Laraine, and she felt a pang somewhere near her heart.

As for Moira, she was her usual self with him, coquettish and sweet. She was accepting a drink and the smile on her lips gradually disappeared when she saw Laraine.

'You didn't say Laraine was coming to lunch, darling,' she accused him.

Margaret said, bending down to kiss her cheek, 'I suggested it. I thought it would be a nice surprise. Besides, it means you can stay all day. Laraine can be company for me while you remain with Charles.'

Moira pouted. 'Thank goodness for that! You don't know how nice it is to feel free from that wretched chair, and being with Charles means I can do just that. He's promised to take me out this afternoon in the car.'

Laraine felt the snub and could not altogether blame the girl after the small scene between them that morning.

She said quietly, 'I can return to Lochdoone if you prefer it, Moira. I understand how you feel.'

To her surprise Moira looked positively furious. 'Don't be so darned accommodating,' she hissed. 'You don't understand at all. No one does.'

'Hey now, that's a bit strong,' admonished Charles. 'No need to be rude to someone who's only doing their job.' His smile at Laraine was the pained one of a man who hated scenes, especially between women. 'After all, the poor girl's job is only a temporary one.'

His light reference to the fact that she would not be there

long filled Laraine with a hurt far greater than the one Moira had inflicted. He seemed to find a certain pleasure in reminding her that she was only a passing acquaintance to him. Her hand shook slightly as she accepted the glass of apple juice that he offered. The time for her departure could not come too quickly for her.

It was comforting to feel Margaret's arm slide around her waist when she came forward to take a glass of sherry from Charles.

'Shall we all sit down at the table?' she asked. 'I can see Jock fidgeting for us to start.'

Jock was near to the sideboard and the silver dishes which he was to serve, and he gave them a sheepish smile. His wink at Laraine did much to restore her confidence, and Charles picked Moira up to carry her to the table. His deep baritone voice rose softly as he sang.

> 'A doll I can carry,
> The girl that I marry must be.'

But Moira was not amused as he lowered her down gently in her chair against the table. Her arms lingered in their hold around his neck, but she said nastily,

'That doesn't mean a thing, darling. You could carry Laraine just as easily as me!'

Charles raised a tantalising brow. His mocking glance slid over Laraine as she took her seat opposite to them across the table, and to her annoyance the heat rose in her cheeks beneath his scrutiny.

Unperturbed, he said, 'You don't need to remind me. I'd say there's very little difference between you in weight. You're both as light as a feather. By the way, I trust your foot is healed?'

Laraine knew that he was deliberately referring to the time when he had carried her to and from the stream after she had cut her foot. But she decided to be as unconcerned about it as he was.

'Quite healed, thanks,' she said.

She saw disappointment in Moira's face, even a hint of vexation that someone else was taking the limelight from her. Charles singing in her ear had only half mollified her. Laraine's natural sweetness, however, only fostered compassion. She could understand her being jealous. Poor Moira! There were few sensations more shattering than to see one's beloved addressing another woman, and enquiring about her welfare. Not that Charles was interested in herself—far from it. All the same, Laraine decided to be very careful in the future in her dealings with Moira's entourage of men. She had little enough for the moment as it was.

The meal was something Laraine would have avoided if given the chance, but Margaret brought everything back on an even keel by enquiring about Moira's visit to the hospital. Her manner was such that even Moira could not keep up her surliness for long. Margaret was one of those people adept at pouring oil on troubled waters. In her sweet face with its fine McGreyfarne nose and lovely eyes lurked a spirit so serenely set that she seemed to be immune from all outward ignominies. She was still very young at heart, and Laraine felt akin to her in the way that they both did not take people for granted, were always careful of other people's feelings and responded instantly to a sense of humour, however small.

As for Charles, his charm, his laugh, his ready wit, his disturbing gaze were thrusting themselves forcibly against the barriers she had built up between them until her heart responded treacherously, completely.

It was with a feeling of relief mixed with unhappiness that she saw him take Moira off after lunch, carrying her down to his car. Her arms were clasped tightly around his neck and her laugh rang out as he settled her in the front seat. When they had gone Margaret suggested a fresh brew of coffee which they drank at leisure on the terrace.

'You're not to be hurt by Moira's little tantrums, dear,' she said. 'We have to allow her some outlet for her feelings. I know it isn't necessary to say this because you understand completely about the whole situation. I suppose you wonder why Charles doesn't propose and give her some encouragement to get well? I think by remaining silent he has a far greater hold over her. She just can't do what she likes with him and she has to behave.'

Listening to her, Laraine felt hollow despite the lunch. Sitting there on the terrace with the song of the birds mingling with the humming of bees among the flowers, she tried to let the peace of it all wash over her. Like Charles, McGreyfarne seemed to grow on her, reaching out tentacles that could imprison her heart and mind for ever. She had no right to fall in love with the place, much less to fall in love with Charles.

Yet how could she be in love with a man whom she hated one moment and longed for the next? She could leave, give in her notice. But would it be fair to Moira? Moira would not be sorry to see her go. The snag was that her going would put the girl in a bad light because her behaviour had forced her to do so. The alternative was to face a situation that was becoming intolerable, with the weeks ahead serving as a period of waiting until such time as her departure was in the end inevitable. But even that would be welcome as long as her departure was not on an intolerable sense of failure. In that moment Laraine felt as keenly as Moira herself the desire for her to walk again.

Margaret had stopped talking and was waiting for an answer. Laraine came out of her thoughts and said gratefully, 'I am enjoying this wonderful morning with you in a way, although I must confess that there's also a faint tinge of unhappiness about Moira and the fact that I'm falling in love with this lovely house.'

'And you aren't too upset about Moira's treatment of you?'

'It was one of the things I expected when I accepted the job. It wouldn't be natural for her to be all sweetness and light, fastened as she is to a wheelchair. And I do appreciate your concern for me.'

'My dear Laraine, I've grown very fond of you, and it will give me the greatest pleasure if you will pay us a visit from time to time when your job with Moira is over.'

But Laraine's murmured 'thank you' was only a matter of politeness, since she knew that it would be impossible for her ever to return to McGreyfarne when Moira was Charles' wife.

When the last of the coffee had been drunk Margaret suggested a stroll down to the sea. They had left McGreyfarne and taken the path over sand dunes thick with spiky marram grass intermingled with blue harebells and green gorse to eventually reach the golden beaches.

'I remember bringing Charles down here when he was a small boy,' mused Margaret. 'He would awaken me at an unearthly hour for us to go down to the beach to watch the fishing boats heading back to the ports along the skyline. He loved to see the lighthouse still flashing a warning and would crouch for hours behind the sand dunes to see the young wild ducks flying overhead as the older ones taught them to fly in formation.'

A tender feeling caught idiotically in Laraine's throat. 'You were very close to him?'

Margaret laughed. 'I had to be. There's only a few years between us. Come, I'll show you the caves where we used to play, and have picnics.'

They climbed up slopes bright with sunlight and flowers. Overhead the vast old trees grew denser with foliage shutting them in. The path, little used now, was almost covered with fern and undergrowth.

'Be careful how you tread,' warned Margaret as she led the way. 'The entrance to the caves is completely hidden.'

Laraine was glad that it was daylight. She did not fancy being alone there in the dark hours. Then Margaret was parting the bushes to reveal the entrance to a dark cavern echoing eerily with their voices.

'Rather spooky, isn't it?' she said brightly. 'Charles used to love to come here to conjure up stories of pirates with cutlasses and evil eyes. He didn't know what fear was and poured scorn on anyone who showed any sign of it. He said that no matter how afraid you were, you had to remember that you were a McGreyfarne, and must never run. That was his philosophy, and he stuck to it.'

Laraine shivered in the dark atmosphere. 'Is there a way out of the cave other than this front entrance?' she queried, envying the older woman's association with Charles as a small boy. It was a part of him that she herself would never know. It was easy to imagine him striding along in a youthful, lordly fashion even through this very cave.

Margaret said, 'There is another way out. Charles knows it well, but we would need a torch to find it. I don't know about you, but I feel like a rest.'

A short distance from the cave they turned a corner, bringing them to a drop far above the sea. A flat jutting ledge formed an inviting and sheltered spot with great tilted rocks on either side forming a sheltered seat hewn out of rock where they could enjoy a panoramic view of sea and sky. They sat down gratefully.

It was a day of southerly weather with the warm breeze tempered by the high altitude. Land and sea were endowed with warmth, colour and dazzling light—the grasses whispering, the rocks warm to the touch with the mingling scents of sea, gorse and crushed fern until every breath was like a drink of wild perfumed nectar.

Laraine inhaled deeply, closing her eyes to feel the warmth of the sun on her face. In her heart was a profound love for the wild untouched country which she felt had taken her to its heart. Gradually her breathing, deep and even, was at one with Margaret's, and silence reigned.

The freshening of the winds awoke her with an unpleasant start. Far below the sea lay dark and menacing while above mountains of clouds nudged each other with the distant clap of thunder. The wind was heavy with the scent of rain, causing her to sit up in alarm.

'Wake up, Margaret,' she cried. 'We're in for a storm. Look at the sky and that sea!'

Margaret opened sleepy eyes, looked dazed for a moment, then sat up, suddenly fully alert.

'We'd better go back to the caves to shelter. It's about to start at any moment. Wow, here it is!' she exclaimed. 'Hurry!'

In that moment the heavens opened and in the scramble to the caves they were drenched. Fortunately they were well under cover, but it was cold and dank from the undergrowth around and they felt uncomfortably chilled.

The rain lasted for well over an hour. Then the sun came out, but it was some time before they ventured out to survey the still menacing sky.

Margaret said wisely, 'I suggest we make tracks for home before the next shower. There's a short cut down the slope here to the beach. If we go back the way we came it will take much longer because we shall be walking knee-deep in wet undergrowth. I vote for this short cut down to the beach. I know it looks awfully steep, but there's a path somewhere that kind of zigzags down. We used to use it years ago. The trouble is finding it.' She moved closer to the edge of the slope. 'I have an idea it's somewhere here . . .'

The next moment, to Laraine's horror, Margaret suddenly disappeared feet first down the steep slope, having slipped on the wet grass covering the edge. For one horrifying moment Laraine stood paralysed with shock. Then she was staring down from what seemed to be a terrifying height to see Margaret huddled half under a clump of gorse, which mercifully had checked her descent midway down the slope.

'Hold on, Margaret, I'm coming!' she called.

For one hair-raising moment fear caught her by the throat at the thought of clambering down the steep slippery slope. She paused to look around helplessly for the path Margaret had mentioned and saw it very much to the right of where Margaret lay. Even if she found where it began every step down would take her further away from her.

There was nothing else for it. Margaret could be badly injured and time was important. Taking the long way round would take too long, especially as the sky was growing more threatening with further rain in the offing.

Laraine sat down on the edge of the drop, dug her heels in desperately into the wet grass and reached out to grip a young oak sapling. The latter yielded for one horrible moment, but it held firm. She began the perilous descent with her heart in her mouth in case of a false move and the rumbling of thunder shaking the very earth beneath her.

It seemed to take years. Her hands were smarting through grabbing at rocks, roots or anything that would help her when finally she slid down the last bit of incline to where Margaret lay. She was on her back, lying submerged beneath the gorse bush from which she was trying unsuccessfully to extricate herself.

'Are you all right?' Laraine bent over her and tried to joke. 'You might have told me you were going to take off down the slope,' she said lightly. 'You scared the daylights out of me!'

Margaret gave a pale smile. 'Sorry. Can you give me a hand to help me to wriggle out of this bush? My left foot is fast among the roots, I think.'

It was no easy matter to release the foot, but when Laraine did by clearing a way around it, and pulling Margaret free, the ankle was very swollen.

'Looks like a bad sprain,' she said.

Margaret felt around the swelling and grimaced with pain. 'I've probably twisted it. By the way, how did you get down so quickly?'

'The same way as you did. You aren't the only one who can scale a steep slope in one minute flat.' Laraine smiled to hide her concern. 'I must confess, though, I didn't break your record. But I did it.'

Laraine moved to put her hands behind her, but she was too late. Margaret, seeing them, gave a cry of dismay. 'Your poor hands, they're bleeding, and here am I worrying about a sprained ankle!'

Taking hold of the scarred dirty hands, she kissed them.

'Bless you, my dear, for what you've done,' she said with some emotion. 'I'm afraid I shan't be able to get far on this ankle.'

Laraine indicated the path some way to their right across rough grass. It was a considerable distance away. 'We have to make our way to it. It's the only way we can go to reach some kind of shelter. You can lean on me down the path. I'm not leaving you to face another storm.'

But Margaret shook her head. 'I refuse to let you go further in risking your life for me. So I'm not going with you to double that risk. You go for help and I'll close my eyes and pray until you reach the path.'

But Laraine was equally determined. She said quietly, 'If you come with me both of us will have more courage and once we've reached the path we can make it to the beach. Come on, let's go.'

The inch-by-inch shuffle across the slope seemed to go on for ever when stones dislodged by their progress went rattling down below them. It made matters worse when heavy drops of rain began to fall again, making their progress more hazardous than ever. The rain was coming down in torrents when they finally reached the path. The going down was a nightmare, with Laraine supporting Margaret and bearing most of her weight as she hopped along on one foot. Apart from the rain making the earth path slippery it trickled down their faces and plastered their already torn clothes to their bodies. The storm was also responsible for not a soul being in sight on the beach below whom they could signal to for help.

Laraine never could recall the exact moment when she reached the point of utter exhaustion. It seemed to come when it did not seem to matter whether they found shelter or not. In fact nothing seemed to matter any more. Battered by the rain and crushed beneath her companion's ever-increasing weight as she clung with an arm around her neck, Laraine was hardly aware of her feet shuffling along. Everything was fading away around her, with only the insistent lashing of the rain against her face smacking her into consciousness. It was several moments before she realised that they were walking on level ground and had reached the blessed safety of the beach. The figures suddenly material-ising in front of them did not register for a moment, but the blessed relief of Margaret's weight being taken from her was a bliss that was encompassed in a complete blackout.

CHAPTER NINE

LARAINE opened her eyes. She recalled opening them once before, but that could have been in another world — a confused world with Morag somewhere near slipping off her wet things and helping her into a nightdress. Too exhausted to bother about it, she had closed her eyes again on feeling the warm luxury of a soft bed and had just floated away. Now she was feeling more normal again except for the terrible ache in her shoulder muscles from supporting Margaret's weight.

Looking round the room brought her back to the present with a jerk, an unpleasant one since she was back in the bed of her room at McGreyfarne. All was silent. Her wrist was bare of her watch, and heaving herself up in bed Laraine looked around for it in vain. It was not on the bedside table, so it was possible that she had lost it while supporting Margaret down to the beach. Ah well, no use thinking about it now, but she would miss it. Harvey had bought it for her on her last birthday—the only expensive gift she had accepted from him among the many that he had offered. He had had their names inscribed inside the back cover. Maybe that it was one good thing to come out of the whole unfortunate incident, since it severed the last tie between them, even if it had been a splendid timekeeper.

Morag entered the room as she was guessing what time it was. The aroma of coffee coming from the tray she carried smelled good.

'Your breakfast, lassie,' said Morag. 'How are you feeling?'

'Fine, thanks,' answered Laraine, trying not to wince at the pain in her shoulders as she pushed herself higher up in bed. 'How is Margaret?'

127

'Not too bad apart from the sprained ankle, and in far better shape than you were last night when Charles carried you up to this very room. You were in a sorry state and no mistake!'

Laraine watched her bend forward to place the tray in front of her.

'Did you say Charles brought me here?' she queried in dismay.

'Aye. Mr Frazer had charge of Margaret. He came over from Lochdoone after Charles had enquired from him about your whereabouts. You see, he and the poor lassie came home early from their outing because of the storm to find you both out. He became concerned as the afternoon wore on and you didn't return, so he and Mr Frazer set out to look for you. We were so relieved when they brought you back, I can tell you.'

Laraine listened in dismay, wondering miserably why it had to be Charles who had carried her back instead of George. George might even have taken her back to Lochdoone, which would have been unlikely since it was farther away. Even so it was hateful to feel obliged to Charles, who certainly would not welcome her as a visitor again to this home. And there was Moira, who would not take kindly to what had happened since it involved Charles in her rescue. Consequently Laraine looked forward to her coming with a taut expectancy which was absurd.

When Morag came to take away her breakfast tray she carried a large cardboard box which she put down upon the bed.

'These are clothes here, lassie, for you to put on,' she said kindly. 'Your own were completely ruined yesterday, and it was a fine thing that you did in taking care of Margaret. Bless you.' There were tears in her eyes. 'She will be coming in to see you later, Moira too. Sure you don't want me to help you wash and dress?'

Laraine shook her head. 'I'm perfectly all right, Morag, thanks, and I only did what anyone else would have done.

Thanks for bringing the clothes from Lochdoone.'

Morag had gone when she opened the box, to find new expensive lingerie and a delightful model dress that she stared at in bewilderment. Where were her own clothes, and why these—all in her size too and obviously selected with care? Then it occurred to her that they could belong to Moira, who had loaned them to her. It was all very strange, and since it was not her intention to ring again for Morag to add to her duties, Laraine decided to wash and put them on. Explanations could come later.

The lingerie was exquisite, with the soft magic of having been the sole work of a silkworm, and the dress, cool and enchanting, was a delight. The material had a faintly designed pattern of flowers on a white background with a cool low neckline. The full skirt enhanced her slender waist as she fastened the narrow matching belt around it. Laraine stared at her reflection in the mirror with a faint surprise at the difference expensive model dresses made to one's whole appearance. Even the poise of her head and the line of her slender neck seemed to take the eye as never before. The revelation was an exciting one, particularly as Laraine had never regarded herself as having any particular attraction for the opposite sex.

There was Charles, the powerful and vibrant master of McGreyfarne. What would he think of her transformation? Steady now, a voice whispered inside her. He belongs to Moira. This sudden thought steadied her pulse down to normal. Every feeling she had for Charles, and most of it sprang unbidden from a treacherous heart, must be quelled before it could prove fatal. Certainly she had not imagined in her wildest dreams that the combination of a man's powerful frame, his voice, a tartan cap set flat on thick fair hair above disapproving fine eyes, could have all served to fill her with the kind of shattering emotion that shuts out common sense. Would it have been any different had they met in London? At a party? At the house of a friend? Laraine argued that it wouldn't. The attraction would still

have been there. The magic making the blood dash madly
through her veins, the breathless feeling at his approach
would have been just as dramatic and real as it was now.
But it just could not be. With this in mind she felt calmer
and chided herself for being such a fool.

She was ready when Margaret and Moira came in,
Margaret sitting on Moira's knee in the wheelchair.

Margaret laughed, 'Behold two of us now indisposed,
and how dare you stand there looking so lovely and enchanting after what we went through yesterday?'

Laraine laughed too and darted forward to help the older
woman to slide off Moira's knee on to a chair nearby.

'Never mind the dress for a moment,' she said. 'How's
the ankle?'

Hurriedly she dragged another chair forward for Margaret to rest her foot on, then sat down on the bed.

'Painful, but I can manage to hobble about on it,' Margaret admitted. 'Charles says I've sprained it, but not too
badly. He thinks I've twisted my knee, and he's sent for the
doctor to give you and me a check-up.'

'But why me?' Laraine exclaimed.

Margaret shrugged. 'Just to make sure you didn't strain
yourself. I'll never know how a slip of a thing like you
managed to half carry me down that slippery path like you
did.'

'But you aren't much heavier than me yourself, and don't
try to make me out a heroine. I won't have it. I only did
what anyone else would have done,' Laraine said firmly.

'Well, I must say your recovery has been rapid,' Margaret observed thoughtfully. 'You look stunning in that
dress. Wouldn't you agree, Moira?'

Moira was less enthusiastic. 'It's the dress.'

'Up to a point, yes,' Margaret agreed. 'I've always
thought that our Laraine was a natural when it came to style
and poise, but the effect of that dress is enchanting if not
startling.' She laughed. 'I'm very glad too if it will divert
some of Charles' anger against me into other channels.'

Laraine said, 'What anger?'

'Charles is angry with me for taking you into danger yesterday. I told him how brave you'd been risking your life down that treacherous slope to reach me after I fell, and how you insisted upon helping me down that wretched slippery path to the beach. It was all my fault, and I'm sorry for the ordeal I forced you through.'

'Nonsense,' Laraine exclaimed. 'We were in it together. Accidents can happen to anyone. Besides, your ordeal was greater than mine. You had an awful shock falling over the edge of the slope and landing painfully in that gorse bush. You also sprained your ankle—something that I was spared.'

Margaret shook her head. 'No matter what you say, Laraine, I owe you a debt I can never repay. But for you I could have been lying there for some time in torrential rain and probably ended up with pneumonia or something equally nasty.'

'You owe me nothing,' Laraine said hastily, then stopped as a thought occurred to her. 'You ... didn't buy me these clothes I'm wearing, did you?' she added warily.

'Not guilty,' Margaret said with a smile.

'Then they must be Moira's.' Laraine's smile at the girl was sweet. 'It's very kind of you to lend me your things, but you could have brought mine from Lochdoone.'

Moira, who had remained silent throughout, looked anything but in a light mood. 'I haven't the least idea what you're talking about,' she said. 'I've certainly never owned a dress like that one you're wearing. Perhaps my father bought it for you, though if he did I wasn't consulted at all. He did it without my knowledge.'

A peremptory tap on the door brought the conversation to a halt as Charles entered, accompanied by a middle-aged man with receding red hair.

'Here they are, doctor, three beautiful girls all waiting for you,' said Charles, looking at them with an easy masterful smile. His height, the width of his shoulders, the brightness of his hair, seemed momentarily to Laraine to shut out the surroundings. His glance over her slim form was enigmatic as he added, 'I don't believe you've met Miss Laraine Winters, Moira's companion, Doctor Convery.'

Laraine had risen from the bed and came forward to shake hands with the rather shabby middle-aged man with a benign smile like a father.

'I agree with you, Charles—a beautiful bevy of girls indeed, and Miss Winters has the look of someone who thrives on ordeals, or are you behaving as if you did?'

The doctor smiled at her appraisingly. The way he had said *gurrls* made her smile. She felt drawn to him at once. He was the perfect family doctor who instilled confidence and seemed in no hurry to push his patients off. One felt that he was very popular among the local people.

'I'm quite all right, doctor ...' she began, then had to turn away hurriedly to give an unexpected sneeze. 'Excuse me,' she added as someone thrust a large white handkerchief into her hand. Her murmured thanks was for Charles, whose handkerchief was offered.

Doctor Convery raised an eyebrow, his regard purely professional.

'No doubt you've caught a chill, Miss Winters,' he said dryly, 'and those scratches on your hands want attending to. What about the shoulder? I believe you took most of Margaret's weight on your unfortunate outing yesterday.'

'Laraine was wonderful, Doctor Convery,' cut in Margaret. 'But for her I could be in hospital with pneumonia. We were both drenched to the skin.'

The doctor's hands were busy manipulating Laraine's shoulder muscles and she winced with pain. His probing fingers seemed to touch on the root of the pain and gradually it eased. He said that all she needed was rest and plenty of good food to combat the chill she had caught. Then he passed on to Margaret.

It was then that Laraine noticed that Charles and Moira had left the room. It was impossible to say just then which of her emotions were the most shattering—relief, pain, jealousy, loneliness—or hurt pride because Charles refused to show any interest in her?

Laraine sat down on the bed with her emotions in a whirl. Moira had probably insisted upon him taking her out somewhere, and he had gone willingly enough for no man allows a woman to use him unless he wishes it. Strangely enough her heart ached for him. Why it did she had not the faintest idea, because no one was more capable of taking care of himself than Charles McGreyfarne. She glanced around the familiar room, aware of how fond she had become of it. Margaret was responsible partly for her feeling of being at home. She was such a wonderful person. The doctor was now examining her kneecap and her low sweet laugh rang out as he tapped her knee. Laraine thought, there's something reminiscent of Charles about her, and she wished she had known his mother.

It was nearing lunchtime when the doctor left. In his opinion Margaret had twisted her ankle and her knee, but neither too seriously. They would improve with plenty of rest. She was to sit and keep her foot up as much as possible during the next few days, and he also stressed the fact that Laraine must also rest and keep free from chills.

Neither Charles nor Moira put in an appearance at lunch, so they dined upstairs in Margaret's sitting room to save her hobbling downstairs. The afternoon was spent in Margaret's workroom, where Laraine acted as a model while Moira's dress was finished. Laraine stroked the elegant folds of the skirt as she turned to all angles for Margaret to give the dress a last critical look. The result was a really breathtaking gown.

While they worked Laraine thought constantly of the outfit she was wearing since that morning. It niggled to know that there was a mystery about where it had come from. But there was nothing to be done until she was back again at Lochdoone, where she could ask Moira's father about it.

'There, that's it.' Margaret spoke with some satisfaction when the work was done. 'You've been a great help, Laraine. Without you I would never have achieved a perfect fit. I'm afraid I've kept you in all day out of the fresh air. I know, why don't you go out now for a short stroll before tea?'

Laraine breathed in luxuriously as she left the house; the perfumed air on her face, and in her heart an ecstasy of love for nature and all her miracles. It was a glorious afternoon of warm golden sunshine and her steps took her along the driveway and out on to the road. She was going to look for her wristwatch. She had made no mention of it to Margaret in case she blamed herself for its loss. And it was not as though the watch was of sentimental value, something Margaret would immediately assume. The trouble was that it had been such an excellent timekeeper, which made it indispensable. However, there was little hope of recovering it since it was not quite clear exactly where she had lost it. She remembered it being on her wrist when she was scrambling down the slope to Margaret, and later when they had reached the path leading to the beach.

A cluster of lazy white clouds floated against a blue sky and the sea air sweeping across the dunes was nectar. A lone heron beat the sky with its wings way above her and a rabbit dashed across the golf course devoid of players. There were quite a few people on the beach, though, as she made her way across it to the path leading up the slopes. It wound round in long snakelike curves among the undergrowth and her watch could have fallen anywhere. Leisurely she strolled on and up, parting the dense fern with a long piece of broken branch picked up at random. It was a hopeless task as she had guessed it would be, but she kept doggedly on until a sense of tiredness crept over her. It was more like exhaustion that made her look for anything in the form of a seat where she could rest for a while. And there it was at the side of the path, a large slab of rock, sunwarmed and inviting. Curling up on it, Laraine laid her head on her arm.

The next thing she knew was the dragging movement of a warm moist tongue on her face. Opening her eyes, she uncoiled herself and sat up to see Mac, who began to lick her hands. There was a movement on the path and her head turned on a sudden awareness.

'Hello,' said Charles.

'Hello,' she answered, gathering her wits sufficiently enough to speak calmly.

In the inevitable silence which followed, his eyes, dark and enigmatic, moved over her deliberately, as she fondled Mac with quivering hands.

'Not ill, are you?' he asked sharply, then hurried on, 'In heaven's name, what are you doing all the way up here after your unfortunate experience yesterday? What are you—a glutton for punishment? Or did you have a reason for coming? This is hardly the time to perform a feat of strength.'

'I came out for a walk,' she answered. 'I sat down to rest and fell asleep.'

'I'm not surprised,' he ventured sardonically. 'You look all in. Too bad you didn't find what you were looking for— it might have been worth it if you had.'

Laraine buried the fingers of a hand in Mac's thick fur, thankful for his comforting presence. She bit her lip.

'I don't know what you mean,' she said in a low voice.

'No? Did it mean so much to you?'

'I ... I haven't the least idea what you're talking about,' she shot at him. Then, uncertainly, 'And I don't understand how you come to be here. Did you come to look for me?'

He said dryly, 'Have you any idea what time it is?'

'No.'

'It's after seven.'

'Surely not?'

He went on, 'Margaret was worried since your stroll was taking so long. Why didn't you tell her where you were going?'

She looked at him bewilderedly. 'But I just drifted up this way. I didn't intend to stay out so late, and I wouldn't worry your aunt unnecessarily.'

She looked up at him to see the grim set of his mouth, the

almost cruel gleam in his eyes. He looked furiously angry. Why? Because he had to look for her again? Was his dislike of her so great that it was turning into more—hate, for instance? Surely not. Laraine quivered beneath his cold gaze.

'No? Not even for this?' he demanded.

Thrusting a hand forward which moments before had been slipped loosely into the pocket of his jacket, he opened it palm upwards. For speechless moments Laraine stared down at her wristwatch. Her throat felt dry and she moistened her lips.

'But it's my watch.' Her voice was almost a croak in her surprise. 'Where did you find it?'

'Caught on my jacket after I'd carried you upstairs to your room and was lowering you down on the bed yesterday.'

'But I don't understand. Why didn't you put it down on the bedside table or even let me know that you'd found it?' Laraine suddenly felt her bewilderment turning into anger. 'If this is another way of getting at me then I don't think much of it. Do you know what I think? I think you're the most detestable man I've ever had the misfortune to meet. Of course, it had to be you who found it. It must have given you great satisfaction to keep quiet about it.'

He shrugged her statement off as being of no consequence and the subtle sarcasm in his voice was marked. 'You are free to express your opinion of me and draw your own conclusions as to my motives. However, here is your watch, safe and sound again—or should I say intact with the loving inscription inside and all?' He moved nearer to bend over her, shoving Mac away with the gentle movement of an arm. 'Allow me.'

Before she could do anything he had taken hold of her slender wrist, and slipped the watch in place.

Laraine retreated imperceptibly from his special brand of masculine fragrance, that of good grooming, a faint masculine awareness of aftershave lotion blended with the aroma of a good cigar. The watch was on her wrist, but she would rather have lost it a thousand times than to be beholden to him for it. Thanks were in order, but they stuck in her throat.

'Thanks,' she said at last, the tears not far away. 'And thanks for all you did yesterday.' She bit her lip as he straightened away from her suddenly. Then she went on, 'You were right when you implied that my coming would bring trouble. If I hadn't been here your aunt wouldn't have gone to the caves and we wouldn't have been caught in the storm. But ... but ... I can't help thinking that your attitude towards me hasn't helped.'

At this point Mac took it into his head to give her a reassuring lick and she put her arm around him to give him a squeeze. The spontaneous action restored some of her calm.

'Sometimes I prefer animals to people,' she said. 'Shall we go?'

His reply was a short mocking bow. 'Agreed.'

Even as he bent to give her a hand in getting to her feet, Laraine was up, and they walked down the path with Mac running ahead. Neither of them spoke on the way back to McGreyfarne.

They were on the drive when she asked, 'Is Moira here? I'd like to know because of returning to Lochdoone.'

'Moira is here,' said Charles, nothing more.

They parted at the entrance of McGreyfarne, Charles with Mac at his heel. Laraine was crossing the hall on her way upstairs when Moira appeared in her wheelchair from the direction of the lounge.

She had changed for dinner that evening into a halter-necked gown in fine cinnamon jersey. Her bare shoulders rose smooth and gleaming, her face was freshly and carefully made up, and she had the look of a young country hostess awaiting her husband's guests. But her eyes were hard, her red lips in a bitter line.

'Nice to see you again,' she said harshly. 'What happened this time?'

Laraine met her morose mood lightly as she usually did, hoping to shake her out of it.

'Nothing really,' she answered with a smile. 'I went for a walk, sat down for a rest and fell asleep. I'm sorry I'm late.' She gave a small laugh of tenderness as she recalled it. 'Mac woke me by licking my face.'

'Dear, dear, that must have been a disappointment when you were expecting the Prince to awaken you with a kiss—or should I say Charles? But you're doing very well. Sorry you're to dine upstairs with Margaret this evening, but I'm sure you won't grudge me some little time with my intended,' Moira's voice was honey-sweet, 'having had so much of his attention these last few days.'

'Charles' attention?' pale-lipped.

'Yes, Charles' attention. I must admire the way you do it.'

Something stabbed at Laraine's heart. She was bewildered, hurt and completely taken aback. 'Do what?' she queried hoarsely.

'Turn everything to your own advantage. You know what I mean, surely? The helpless heroine—so pathetic!'

Moira's eyes were twin daggers of jealousy. There was no subtlety in her. She came right out with what she thought regardless of how she hurt. It was certainly embarrassing to be on the receiving end, but, in Laraine's opinion, it made things easier all round. You knew where you stood with her.

So she looked at her steadily, trying not to flinch before so much hate, and said quietly, 'You know that isn't true.'

'Do I?'

'Yes, you do,' firmly.

Moira propelled herself nearer, silently, menacingly. 'I know something that's true—you're in love with Charles.' I've watched you when you've been in his company. You've avoided meeting his eyes too often for it not to be noticed.

I've been waiting for this opportunity to confront you with it.' Her nostrils quivered with anger. 'When he gave you your wristwatch did you kiss him or did he kiss you?'

She glared at the watch as Laraine lifted a hand to her hot face. Withdrawing imperceptibly, pale now with hurt and disgust, she said,

'What do you know about my watch?'

'Only that Charles sent it to town yesterday to have the fastening strengthened, and that he collected it this afternoon while we were out.'

Laraine was completely shaken. 'Oh no!' she cried.

'Oh yes!' mocked Moira. 'You've been too romantic for words. Pity it's all wasted, since Charles belongs to me. I know we're in a rather vague situation at the moment, but I have first claim. We might have been married now had I not gone to London and had this stupid accident. Anyway, I don't even have to hint at a possible engagement—everybody including Father and Margaret believes it. The staff expect it. So you see you're only wasting your time.'

Laraine clenched her hands by her sides. To be drawn in a free-for-all fight over a man was too frightful to contemplate, and with someone as helpless as Moira it seemed odious and despicable. With her head held high she kept her steady frank gaze on Moira's distorted face, and said nothing. Her eyes did it for her. Steadfastly her naturally sweet, compassionate nature refused to allow her to hit at someone who was down. Moira sat there in all her loveliness, absolutely queen of the situation, but Laraine only saw the poor helpless legs beneath.

It was Moira who had to lower her eyes first, and Laraine walked slowly across the hall to the staircase. She had reached the bottom step when Moira hissed, 'Ask Charles where your dress came from. But don't kid yourself as to the reason he bought it. He did so out of gratitude for what you did for his aunt. He adores her. Besides, he didn't like being in your debt—he told me so.'

Laraine stumbled up the first step of the stairs and laid a

hand for a moment on the top of the carved post of the balustrade. She might have known that George could not have bought it. He would naturally have sent some of her clothes from Lochdoone. Mechanically, Laraine made her way to her room. She washed her face and hands, combed her hair and applied fresh make-up. Thank goodness she had nothing to change into for dinner with Margaret—not that it was necessary. She ought to be grateful to Moira for sparing her from meeting Charles again, much less dining with him that evening. She had more than enough of Charles and guessed that he felt the same way about herself.

Futilely she wished now that she had stayed in bed all day. It was what she had needed to get over her ordeal of the previous afternoon, and she would have been spared the scene with Moira, not to mention the encounter with Charles on the slopes. Things had been said to him which were far better left unsaid, scathing things accusing him of keeping her watch for his own sadistic amusement when he had taken it to have the weak catch repaired. It occurred to her then that not only did she owe him for her outfit but also for the repairs to her watch. Well, he would be paid. She would see to that if it was the last thing she did.

Wearily she finished her toilet with a trace of lipstick and looked for a fresh hankie. It was then she saw the handkerchief in her bag that Charles had given her at McGreyfarne when she had sneezed in the presence of the doctor. Impatiently she flung it across the room.

Drat Charles! she thought. Would she never be out of his debt? It was in this state of mind and feeling ready to battle with anything that she whipped up a clean hankie and made her way to Margaret's room.

She never did remember anything clearly about her dinner with Margaret except that she must have put on a good show, since she never guessed that there was anything amiss. At ten o'clock Charles took her back to Lochdoone with Moira. She sat in the back of the car with a wrap borrowed from Margaret to keep out the chill night air. But the chill in her heart was there to stay. Even the sight of Moira's head against Charles' shoulder as he drove made no impression on her. It was just as though something had died inside her.

When they arrived at Lochdoone Laraine left Margaret's wrap in the car and slipped quietly up to her room. It was some time later when she went to Moira's room to find her asleep.

CHAPTER TEN

LARAINE opened her eyes the next morning to the sound of rain pattering on the windows. The skies were not completely overcast, for there were promising patches of blue in between the scudding dark clouds. But for the moment she felt the sensation of being closed in and it gave her a feeling of restlessness. The incidents of the previous day could not be put aside and forgotten. After the scene with Moira some decision had to be reached whether it was sensible for her to stay on in the present untenable position. Her first reaction was to leave immediately sooner than face the accusing jealousy in Moira's eyes. However, that was impossible since there had to be some straight talking between them.

When Mrs Dougal came with her morning cup of tea, she asked with concern, 'How do you feel? That was a dreadful ordeal you went through the other day. You look tired. Dougal and I were worried about you when they telephoned from McGreyfarne to enquire if you were here during that storm.'

Laraine pushed herself up in bed and accepted her tea with a warm smile.

'Thanks,' she said sincerely, 'I'm fine now. In any case I didn't get the worst of it.'

'So I believe.' Mrs Dougal folded her arms across her bosom, ready for a spot of gossip. 'How is Miss McGreyfarne?'

'Improving.' Laraine sipped her tea, reluctant to be drawn into any gossip about people of whom she was so fond. 'I'm going to miss your delightful brew when I go. This tea is delicious.'

If Mrs Dougal was disappointed at being sidetracked from a gossip, she did not show it.

She said, 'Surely you won't be going yet? You're so good for Mr Frazer and his daughter, poor lassie. She didn't sleep too well last night, so she's having a lie-in this morning.'

So that was the attitude Moira was going to take, Laraine thought, after Mrs Dougal had gone. Was it possible that the girl had been feigning sleep when she had called in to see her the previous evening? Not that she blamed her, since a confrontation of the kind they were all set for would have hardly been conducive to a good night's sleep afterwards.

Laraine sighed. What a mess the whole thing was, and far worse for Moira, for whom she still felt a deep compassion. She had no idea where it would all end. She could only do her best and pray that it would all come out right.

George Frazer greeted her cordially enough when she entered the dining room.

'Good morning, my dear,' he said breezily. 'Sorry I happened to be out when you returned last night. How are you feeling after your adventure on the slopes? Charles was really worried about you both, you especially since you went out cold on us. I've never seen a man act so swiftly. Before I'd got a grip on Margaret he had whipped off his jacket and wrapped you in it, and was striding away to where we'd left the car.'

Laraine allowed him to draw a chair out for her at the table, and she sat down.

'I'm so sorry to have done that,' she told him ruefully.

'Nonsense,' he cried indignantly. 'You were a real heroine doing what you did instead of going for the easier way of running for help.' He paused, looked at her more closely. 'You are feeling all right, aren't you?'

'Of course I am. And forget what I did. I would have been a coward to have done otherwise.' Laraine bit her lip, wondering how to begin to say what she had intended, and stared down into the cup of coffee he handed her across the table. Inadvertently he helped.

He said seriously, 'You're one of the nicest people I've

ever had the good fortune to meet. You're so unassuming and at the same time so frank and honest it's a delight to be in your company. You had a rotten time rescuing Margaret, and then if that wasn't enough, my very wayward daughter tore strips off you last night on your return here.'

Laraine felt her colour go. Her hand shook so much that she had to lower her coffee cup back to the table without tasting it.

'I beg your pardon?' she said weakly. 'How did you know about it?'

He shrugged. 'Let's say I was told about it—and not by my daughter either.'

'You mustn't blame Moira,' said Laraine with a strained white look on her face. 'You said just now that I was frank and honest. Well, so is your daughter. She had certain views which she expressed, and don't regard me as having too many virtues. I make as many mistakes as the next person, and I'm afraid . . .'

She broke off, aware of him regarding her earnestly. 'Go on,' he prompted. 'Of what are you afraid?'

Her reply came with great difficulty. 'I'm afraid I made a mistake in coming here. You see, I . . . I didn't foresee the problems I would be faced with. Oh, don't get me wrong—Moira isn't to blame for some of them. In fact she's been very good considering the blow fate has dealt her. I . . . I don't want you to think that my doubts about taking this position are anything to do with her behaviour towards me. Far from it.'

George said quietly, 'So you want to go? Is that it?'

She nodded. 'I think it's wise, don't you?'

'No, I don't. I'll tell you something now. Before you came Moira was giving us a terrible time—the staff and myself, I mean. Now she's drawn her horns in because she's afraid of everyone around her becoming more fond of you than they are of her. Of course, that's nonsense. We all love her, but that's Moira, always so possessive. You have to understand her to love her.'

'I know,' Laraine conceded. 'I'm fond of her too, you know.'

He nodded. 'You have that wonderful capacity to love other people. That's why you're so good for my daughter. Besides, who's going to persuade her to go to Rome to see the specialist if you back out now? I'm counting on you.'

She bit her lip. Common sense told her to go now while there was still time to get the whole thing out of her system. It was hurting too much to allow it to grow into immense proportions. To become further involved was only asking for trouble. Charles had said that one could not be all things to all people. On the other hand, she could try again to persuade Moira to agree to see just one more specialist. Someone had to do that before it was too late. Besides, Charles' whole future happiness depended on Moira walking again, and perhaps Margaret's as well.

At last she admitted slowly, 'I don't mind staying, but only if Moira is agreeable. There's something else too. I don't know how much you know of our quarrel last evening, but she mustn't know that you've been told about it. It will only give her something else to brood on, plus the fact that her behaviour is being commented upon. Nothing nor no one must make her feel more bitter than she does now.'

A slow smile lightened George's worried features. 'You know, you're quite a girl. I agree wholeheartedly. There is one thing, though. I think you deserve a break today. Have you seen my daughter this morning?' He lifted a brow as Laraine shook her head. 'No?' He smiled. 'My guess is that she'll stay out of sight for a while. In the meantime there's no reason why you shouldn't take a break away from it all. Any ideas?'

He cast a jaded eye at the rain-splashed tall windows, and wrinkled his brow in such a way that Laraine had to laugh. It had not occurred to her to ask for time off. Indeed, she had reckoned herself lucky to be at the beck and call of Moira without any thought of a break, and there was one snag.

She said, 'Don't you think we'd better sound your daughter as to whether I'm still welcome here as her companion?'

George gave his head a negative shake.

'You leave that to me,' his eyes smiled warmly on to her serious face. 'I know my daughter. She won't want you to go—you'll leave too big a gap in her life. Neither Charles, Rob or I have the time to be at her beck and call, and poor Margaret is indisposed. Why not go out for the day on a shopping spree? Spend your first pay cheque? I'll send it up to your room after breakfast, then you can go out at your leisure.'

She stammered, 'But I ... haven't been here long enough for a pay cheque and ... and it will be silly to pay me in advance.'

'Nonsense. Your presence here has meant a lot to us all. At least let me give you a little back in exchange for your very valuable help. Now eat your breakfast like a good girl. You may use my car if you wish.'

Laraine digested this and thought quickly, If I'm to get right away I want nothing to remind me of my job. To get on a bus, to travel to places unknown and explore without any thought of Lochdoone or McGreyfarne—that's what I want.

'Thanks,' she said. 'But I would like to use a bus. I suppose I can catch one to town?'

He looked at his watch. 'There's a long-distance one passing through at ten-thirty.'

So it was a little after ten when Laraine emerged from the house to stroll down to the village for the bus. The rain had stopped and the slight coolness in the scented air was very refreshing. There was plenty of room on the bus when it arrived, a comfortable coach containing mostly American tourists, all in good humour. Passing through beautiful country where fine hospitable hotels and pretty cottages advertising bed and breakfast whetted a healthy appetite, Laraine revelled in the history of countryside beloved of Scott,

and the Borderers, and alighted at one of the Border towns
fully prepared to enjoy her day.

Her first visit was to a bank to cash the cheque George
Frazer had given her. She had already planned what to do
with it—pay Charles what she owed him. Her plan was to
post it to him with a short note explaining why. There were
quite a few people in the bank where the cheque was cashed
without difficulty, so it was not surprising that she rubbed
against a big wide-shouldered figure going out between the
swing doors.

'Laraine! What are you doing here?'

Laraine whitened at the deep familiar voice and returned
the steady gaze of Charles. She studied with senses sharpened by a similar encounter the finely cut features, the
tartan cap set flatly on the crisp blond curls, the air of self-
assurance, and pain squeezed her heart as she recalled their
first encounter on her arrival in his beloved country. He
looked very big in the doorway as he drew her out of danger
from the revolving doors out on to the pavement. He wore
riding breeches and an open-necked shirt with a silk paisley
scarf tucked in elegantly against his firm brown throat.

Underneath the tranquillity she had acquired during the
coach journey surprise stirred her senses into something
dangerous and frightening. Her lips parted to show the tips
of white teeth in a warm skin that glowed and the healthy
clearness of her lovely eyes had a dramatic effect had she
but known it.

'I've been given the day off,' she replied lightly, although
her heart was thundering against her ribs.

Afterwards Laraine looked back on those moments and
the way Charles looked down at her as a time that could
not be discounted nor forgotten. In a dream she felt the
light pressure of his hand on her arm, a touch which did not
promise too close a contact as he spoke.

'And how had you planned to use your day?' he asked,
slowing his long stride to accommodate her dainty steps.

Her casual light manner was assumed deliberately to put him off.

'I'm going to amuse myself as only a woman can in browsing around at the delightful shops and perhaps a visit to the woollen and tweed mills later,' she said airily. 'But you as a male wouldn't be interested in such flippant joys.'

'On the contrary,' he replied dryly, 'I have to do a bit of shopping myself for Margaret. Where are you going for lunch?'

The mention of his aunt caused her to give a guilty start.

'How is she?' she asked.

'She's improving and yearning to be on her feet again. And you?'

'Quite well. I want to thank you for all you've done for me.'

It was on the tip of her tongue to mention the debt she was determined to pay, but on second thoughts the safest way to settle the unfortunate affair was to do as she first intended and send him a letter with the money enclosed. That way he would not be able to pit his strength of argument against her own. For he would, there was no doubt of that.

'You didn't answer my question.'

The words cut into her thoughts and warm colour rushed to her face.

'I beg your pardon?' Why, oh, why could she not think of some good excuse—that she was dining with someone else—anyone? But he was no fool. She just could not get out of this one.

'You heard. I asked where you were going for lunch.'

'I haven't decided.' Laraine found herself babbling. 'Probably I—er—I shall have a snack somewhere. After all, I want to see everything and I don't want to waste time eating.'

'You won't find shopping on an empty stomach very exhilarating,' he said harshly. 'I deem it my duty to see that you're properly fed on your day out. You've eaten little enough in the last few days. Come on, I know just the place. And don't look so dismayed at the prospect of dining with me. You'd be surprised how many young ladies have enjoyed my company!'

While she did not doubt this Laraine was worried about how long he would persist in keeping her company even to giving her a lift back home. She had planned on posting her letter to him settling her debt while she was in town. Since she put the money and the note previously addressed to him in an envelope while she had been in the bank, all that remained was for her to post it. But how without his knowledge? It would never do to carry a letter addressed to Charles McGreyfarne back with her to Lochdoone. She came back to the present with a little start.

'I'll take your word for it,' she said. 'I believe I am rather hungry——'. She broke off lamely.

The place Charles took her to was set in a garden ablaze with azaleas and rhododendrons. He stood aside for her to enter the spacious dining room. Flower arrangements stood out enchantingly against softly lit walls, and bloomed in profusion in bright little pots, adding a homely touch to a sophisticated happy scene. For it was happy. Most of the immaculate tables were already occupied by people who were laughing, talking and eating, with several women turning curiously to watch Charles who was piloting Laraine to a corner table across the room by a window.

They dined off freshly caught salmon and salad, then roast beef and vegetables followed by fruit, cheese and coffee. While they ate Charles explained that he was on business in the town and if she did not mind being driven around in a horsebox it would give him great pleasure to take her round all the places of interest. Indeed, he would be grateful to her if she would help him choose material from the mills for his aunt. When he put it like that, Laraine could hardly refuse.

So after lunch they spent time in the local mills where tweed and woollen materials were woven into delightful garments. Charles explained that it was a vital part of the economy of the town, and with Laraine's help he chose tartan and tweed in heather colours with matching knitting wools and lovely cashmere. The girl assistants looked at Charles admiringly, and with undisguised envy at Laraine. He was, of course, charming to them, his smile bringing blushes to young cheeks which he did not appear to notice.

Laraine found herself wishing that he had been as charming to her at their first meeting, then immediately changed her mind about it since his charm had been lethal enough even at his most brusque moments.

The rain had cleared up before lunch and the countryside sparkled with a pristine freshness and the charming little shops displaying pottery, pewter, jewellery and other crafts were very busy with visitors.

They had tea at a delightful little teashop near a gurgling stream where a pretty waitress brought plates of scones, cakes, and delicious Selkirk bannock—a large kind of fruit bun which was a speciality of the Border country. Laraine found the time slipping by far too swiftly and all too soon they were making their way back to where Charles had parked the horsebox.

'Not exactly the kind of thing to go sightseeing in,' Charles remarked. 'I must apologise for it. You don't mind?'

'I'm enjoying it,' Laraine answered, knowing that she would have enjoyed going out with him in a dustcart. She was angry at her sudden rise of colour, but he had not noticed. With his hand on her elbow, he was leading her into a high-class jewellers. Inside he chose a large gem stone pendant on a gold chain—a beautiful gift, and she appraised his choice wryly. No doubt he was an expert on such matters, having chosen similar gifts for his former girl-friends.

He wrote out a cheque while the case was wrapped up, then he put it into his pocket. With a painful tug at her heart, Laraine wondered who he had bought it for, then decided to forget it in a determination to enjoy her day out.

The journey back to Lochdoone in the horsebox gave her the feeling of returning from a ball like Cinderella with only a beautiful memory to look back upon. Charles pointed out interesting landmarks on the way and she listened bemused by his deep brown voice. None of it seemed real. Here was Charles talking to her with no hint of the animosity he had shown hitherto in her company. Dappled sunshine fell across the cab of the horsebox, emphasising the quality of light outlining his strong, arrogant profile. Laraine sat there watching the strong lean hands on the car wheel in a kind of torpor.

'Why are you so unhappy?'

The question came out of the blue, jerking her back to reality like the shot of a pistol.

'What a strange question,' she commented. 'Why on earth should you think I'm unhappy?'

'Because you've changed, my child. That first day I met you at the station you were all eager-eyed to begin your new job. It isn't as easy as you expected, is it? There are problems you didn't expect, are there not?'

Laraine stiffened inwardly, wondering what he was getting at. She said evenly, 'Naturally there are problems, but I'm learning to deal with them.'

'Want any help?'

She bit her lip. 'I appreciate your offer which, incidentally, comes a bit late, but I'm quite capable of doing things my way.'

'You mean any help is not welcome or any help from me?'

'Yes to both,' she replied.

'I'd say you aren't happy about something and are in need of help. If you remember I did warn you how demanding the job might prove to be.'

Her voice, low and husky, came from a downbent head as she stared down at her hands in her lap. Her knuckles were white from clutching her handbag on her knee.

'Yes, you did, but you're the last person I would confide in. I don't think you could help me at all.'

Charles had slowed the horsebox to a crawl and was looking down at her intently. Slowly she lifted her chin and noticed for the first time how well sculptured his mouth was, beautifully so with a slight upward tilt at each corner. Oh yes, he had a sense of humour, but not for Laraine Winters.

He said softly, 'Laraine, I know and you're aware that I know what kind of problems are troubling you. You can't put your feelings into a vacuum because no matter how tight you lock them in they will surface despite all efforts to suppress them. You must have learned that by now.'

That and a great deal more, she thought wryly, with a sudden quiver at his use of her name. The important thing was to play it cool. He could not possibly know how she felt about him, nor about the recent crisis between Moira and herself. Her first reaction was to tell him that she refused to say anything more on the subject. After all, he had probably been working up to this moment of truth or whatever it was in order to derive a certain amount of malicious enjoyment over her discomfiture.

On the other hand, she could be mistaken. He had given her a most enjoyable day. Surely in the circumstances it would be wrong to spoil it by being rude or ungrateful? His motives for being nice to her were his own affair, as her life was hers. In the sudden silence the air seemed fraught with electricity. Then with a swift movement of a hand Charles whipped a small object from his pocket and dropped it into her lap.

'A small present,' he said laconically. 'For helping me this afternoon at the mill.'

Laraine stared down stupidly at the small oblong parcel containing the pretty golden pendant he had purchased a short time ago.

'But I don't want it,' she cried. 'I owe you enough

already. You don't have to pay me for everything I do, as if
... I was an employee of yours. What did you do, sell
another horse to pay for it?'

He glanced at her for a moment, then threw back his head
and roared with laughter. 'Wherever did you get that idea
from?—that I'm hard up?' he said, and sobered at the
glistening of a tear on her cheek. 'You're a funny child. I
give you a present and it makes you cry. You really meant
what you said just now, didn't you, even about my regarding you as an employee?'

'You bet I did. Here, take your gift, and this with it!'

Laraine opened her handbag with shaking fingers, drew
out the letter she intended posting to him and thrust it at
him. There was a short ominous silence as Charles looked
down at it, then he swung the horsebox off the road into a
quiet layby and shut off the engine.

Silently he took the letter, perused the name and address,
glanced at her briefly, then opened it. His brow was like
thunder as he saw the money, then he read the letter.

His voice icy, he said, 'And what is this supposed to
mean?'

'It's what I owe you for the outfit you bought for me
when my own clothes were ruined in the storm.'

He looked puzzled for a moment. 'How did you know I'd
bought them? Who told you?'

Wearily she said, 'Does it matter?'

He laughed. 'You little goose! You thought I couldn't
afford it. How sweet of you!'

'Sweet of me?' she echoed in disgust, brushing away the
tears with a childlike gesture. 'Why shouldn't I hate the
thought of being in your debt as much as you hate the idea
of being in mine?'

His eyes narrowed in a cold gleam. 'What do you mean
by that?' he demanded, turning towards her with an arm on
the wheel of the cab.

The action brought him nearer and she drew back, trying
to keep a dignified front.

She lifted her chin. 'You know what I mean. You bought the clothes to replace those I ruined in the storm the other day. You also had the repair done to my wristwatch because you couldn't bear the thought of being in my debt for what I'd done for your aunt.'

Her voice had trembled despite all her efforts to control it and his anger appeared to soften.

Very quietly, he said, 'I've never said anything to anyone about being in your debt. I don't admit to buying you any clothes either. I'd like to know who told you I had.'

Laraine shrugged wearily. 'What does it matter? The money is there to pay for them. I always pay my debts.'

'Congratulations,' he said sardonically. 'So you had to pay me for what you thought you owed me.'

Savagely he rammed the money, the letter and the pendant in the handbag open on her lap, then clicked it shut. Then he sat looking down at her until she felt like screaming. But she sat there silent.

His anger was back. He was furious and implacable. Reaching out for her shoulders, he gripped them and forced her to face him.

'So you want to pay your debt. Pay it by all means, but it will be my way. I don't suppose you will enjoy it any more than I shall, but at least the matter will be over and done with. You can give me a kiss in payment. It's what a girl usually gives to a man who makes her a gift.'

His face seemed to draw nearer through a mist as he smiled with a chilling coldness. The blood pounded through her veins. She thought with terror, I wanted this although it terrifies me, and it must not be. She tried to hold him off with her hands, but they might have been wings beating futilely against the bars of a cage. Her voice had gone. It was like being drawn close to a furnace, an agony yet a joy, as Charles bent his head to force her lips to the will of his. The passion of his anger rushed out in a white heat that took her breath. He was all cruel strength, punishing lips, and bone-cracking arms whipped tightly around her.

When he released her, Laraine was like one who had been shocked out of her senses, pain and ecstasy together. Her bruised lips trembled at the thought. She was hardly aware of him starting the engine, and a few minutes later, formally, coldly, Charles dropped her off at the door of Lochdoone.

CHAPTER ELEVEN

LARAINE stood by the window of her bedroom for once not seeing the enchanting view, trying to sort out her confused thoughts—reviewing her own position at Lochdoone in the light of what had happened. Her heart ached with despair, but her problems had to be faced. As far as she could gather Charles had driven away as soon as he had dropped her off at the door. There had been no sign of Moira or her father when she had made her way upstairs. They could be out. Pain at the thought of what Charles' kiss had meant to her laid deep shadows in her eyes.

Taking a long breath, a long quivering sigh rising from the secret recesses of her heart, Laraine shrugged off the memory of his controlled, expressionless face and set about getting herself ready for dinner that evening.

George Frazer was at the sideboard when she entered the dining room, and he turned with a bottle in his hand.

'Hello there,' he smiled. 'Just in time for a drink. Did you have a nice day?'

Laraine sat down and smiled at him, thinking that he looked much brighter than he had done of late.

'Yes, thanks, I enjoyed it immensely. I visited the woollen mills and the enchanting shops with their quaint gifts. Scotland is like England in that respect. It's always a great pleasure to go shopping.'

She accepted her apple juice politely, aware that she had been babbling. But her host saw nothing amiss. He poured himself a drink and lifting it said, 'Cheers.' After he had drunk he looked at her a little curiously. 'You look rather tired. Didn't overdo it, did you?'

She shook her head. 'Shopping is tiring, though in a nice way.'

'As long as you enjoyed it,' he answered philosophically. 'Not worrying over my daughter, are you? It may surprise you to hear that she's forgotten her quarrel with you. She was quite upset because you'd gone out for the day without her.' He leaned against the side of the fireplace and grinned. 'You'll find her much as usual when she comes down. Rob is dining with us.'

Rob came in and accepted a non-alcoholic drink from George with his usual good humour. Apparently he had been away on business for George and discussed it with him over drinks. When Moira came in she was greeted with silence. She was wearing soiled jeans and a crumpled shirt. It was evident that she wanted to annoy. Her father seemed about to speak, then changed his mind and gave her a drink in silence.

With Laraine she was lukewarm but polite, asked if she had enjoyed her day out and wheeled herself up to the dining table. Rob ignored her after a brief lifting of surprised brows and went on to talk about the cattle auctions he had attended recently. Laraine mentioned the white cattle she had seen on her arrival, and the conversation proved interesting to all but Moira. It was not until Rob refused the wine at dinner that she said maliciously, 'You're becoming quite dull, Rob. No wine? Are you off women too?'

He smiled. 'I have to be, don't I, with no money?'

'That shouldn't stop you,' she said in bored, insolent tones. 'It never used to do.'

Rob's eyes gleamed. 'I'm sorry if I annoy you. I remember a time when you used to regard me as anything but dull. However, you won't be annoyed by my presence much longer.'

It was George who took him up on this surprising remark.

'Not thinking of leaving us, are you, Rob? Surely you are used to Moira's teasing by now,' he remarked mildly.

Moira scoffed, 'Don't tell me that someone else has been misguided enough to offer you a change of job?'

Rob met her eyes levelly. 'However did you guess?' he said with biting sarcasm.

'Now, now, you two, behave yourselves,' George said sternly. 'You're joking, Rob, of course.'

'No, I'm not. My stepfather has offered me a job managing a ranch he's bought in Mexico. If I can make it pay he says it's mine. It's a chance of a lifetime and I'd be a fool to turn it down.'

George's face set. It was clear that this was the last thing he had expected. In the silence which followed Laraine saw Moira go pale. The girl had only toyed with her food, and she now stretched out a hand to a cigarette box beneath her father's disapproving eye. Laraine knew it was done to irritate Rob when she deliberately lighted one.

'Put that out,' commanded her father. 'We haven't finished eating yet. Isn't it enough that you come down looking like a slut? Mind your manners, girl!'

Unused to such treatment from her father, Moira stared for a moment, pressed out the newly lighted cigarette into an ashtray, regained some of her composure, and backing the wheelchair from the table propelled it swiftly from the room.

Laraine felt a lump in her throat, swallowed and said weakly,

'I think I'd better go after her.'

'Stay where you are, Laraine,' George said firmly. 'Moira must learn that she can't do just as she pleases, and I won't have her being rude to my guests.'

She bit her lip and felt compelled to have her say. 'I don't think Rob minded, and I'm sure I didn't. It was rather funny really. It would have been wiser to ignore her instead of blowing your top,' she said.

'You must allow me to be the judge of that. Perhaps I'm lacking in a sense of humour when my daughter embarrasses me at the table and my manager talks of leaving,'

George said cryptically. 'What I can't understand is why you haven't mentioned this before, Rob, instead of springing it on me like this.'

Rob's face coloured and he looked sheepish. 'I intended to tell you this evening,' he murmured. 'I'm sorry it's happened like this. On the other hand, you did make the job for me because of my association with Moira. I think you always felt that she was a little to blame for my wild extravagances in the past. She wasn't, you know. If it hadn't been her it would have been some other girl.'

Laraine was sure that George did not realise that he was doing the very thing for which he had upbraided his daughter, reaching out for a cigarette while they were still eating. Not that it mattered, because none of them seemed to have any appetite. Rob gazed dispassionately down at his plate, and reaching out for the glass of wine he had rejected earlier, tipped it up and drained it. Then Laraine had to laugh. It started with a chuckle and soon she was rocking with laughter. Both men looked at her for a moment as though she had taken leave of her senses, then George looked at his cigarette, Rob looked at the empty wine glass, and both men joined her in hearty laughter, as the penny dropped.

After that, with the air cleared of all tension, they began to pick up the drift of normal conversation. Later, after coffee, George went to his study with Rob, leaving her free to go to Moira. She was not looking forward to it, but after the disturbing events of the day seeing Moira again, even if she was still in one of her bad moods, was nothing to worry about.

Moira was seated in her wheelchair with her back to the door of her room. She was gazing out into the gathering dusk. She was smoking, Laraine noticed with a painful resignation, sensing that the girl's nerves were on edge.

'Hello,' she said gently by way of greeting. 'Are you all right?'

There was no reply. Deliberately Moira inhaled and exhaled from her cigarette, then turned the chair slowly to face the door. Her face was in the shadow, but Laraine would like to bet that she had been crying.

'What if I'm not all right?' she cried fiercely. 'What can you do about it?'

Laraine's colour rose warmly. 'I can give you companionship and a helping hand,' she answered evenly.

'Because Rob is going? That's what you mean, isn't it?' Moira wheeled her chair to the bedside table and stubbed out her cigarette. 'Rob and I have known each other all our lives,' she went on defensively. 'I can't imagine Lochdoone without him. We did everything together—including spending all his money.' She looked up at Laraine as if something had only just struck her. 'You know, I think that was the happiest time of my life, now I come to think about it. After that,' she shrugged carelessly, 'nothing seemed to matter any more. I was just drifting when the accident happened.'

Laraine said softly, 'Maybe it was part of the jigsaw you had to put right. Think what could happen if you tried to walk again. You could marry and have children. Why not see the specialist in Rome?'

Moira shook her head. 'Not that again, please! I'm not going to see any specialist and that's that. I know what the answer will be.'

And no matter how Laraine tried, she refused to change her mind. She had helped her into bed and was massaging her neck and shoulders when Mrs Dougal came with a hot drink.

Laraine was dead tired when eventually she went to her room. But sleep avoided her. Her failure to convince Moira that she was doing wrong in refusing to see a specialist kept going through her mind. Had she used the wrong tactics? Once again she had the conviction of having failed in her job.

Restlessly her thoughts turned to Charles and his savage embrace. Her treacherous heart lifted at the thought of his kisses, and it was a very long time before she drifted into sleep.

Life at Lochdoone was tranquil for the next few days. Moira was subdued but manageable. The weather continued warm and sunny after a short break of sudden showers and they spent their time outdoors with the painting and sketching gear. Rob was leaving at the end of the month. He did not come to dine again and seemed to be avoiding the house. Laraine had seen him from time to time on horseback around the estate, but only at a distance.

Like Charles, he rode well, but Laraine was determined not to think of Charles. Margaret telephoned every day to give a bulletin on her ankle which was almost well again, but her knee was taking longer. It was still painful. Several times she telephoned to make excuses for Charles not going to Lochdoone to see Moira. Pressing business matters were keeping him occupied, but it was only temporary.

Laraine ought to have felt relieved at his absence, but her heart said something different. So it was not surprising that she felt a strange excitement at hearing that the annual hunt ball was to be held this year at McGreyfarne and that they were all expected to attend. The lovely panne velvet skirt and top which she had modelled for Moira was despatched to Lochdoone by Margaret for the occasion. An enclosed note to Moira stated that since her knee was still giving her trouble she would not be joining in the dancing, so she would be looking forward to her coming to keep her company. Laraine guessed that Margaret was making out that her knee was worse than it was in order to have an excuse to sit with Moira. In her compassion the older woman wanted to spare the girl distress at not being able to join in the revelry. The dress she had made as a surprise for Moira fitted her like a dream. The blue and silver background of the panne velvet skirt and georgette top brought out the lovely grey in her eyes, and her shining golden hair completed a picture that made one forget the wheelchair.

Laraine, feeling cool, fresh and radiant after an invigorating time spent under the shower, put on the pastel pink cotton dress, hoping that the rainbow colours would look more in a party mood. The pretty neckline and cap sleeves were ornament enough with the addition of matching rainbow studs in her ears. Her hair, newly shampooed, was silky and curled softly away from her face, and her eyes glowed clear and healthy between thick lashes.

As she had dressed, Laraine thought of Charles. She would have to keep out of his way in order to keep up the barrier that was necessary to keep between them. Since he had kissed her a deep-seated unwillingness to have anything to do with him again had formed itself in her mind. She could not explain why it was, but upon reflection she could only put it down to the dangerous attraction he held for her, that deep penetrating gaze he had that reached her heart with all the disconcerting swiftness of a surgeon with a scalpel.

Rob accompanied them to McGreyfarne, carrying the wheelchair to the big car while George conveyed his daughter to the front seat beside him. Laraine thought both men looked attractive and clan-conscious in their kilts, which they wore with an air. In her opinion the wearing of the kilt increased the almost primitive masculinity these fine men from the Border country seemed to convey.

As they set out the light was imperceptibly changing. After a day of golden sunshine a luminous glow lit the heavens spreading softly as it strengthened to spill muted beauty over the countryside. Laraine glanced at Rob as he sat beside her staring out silently as though his thoughts were miles away. Was he unhappy to be leaving his country, or was he just yearning to be gone? Whichever it was it was sufficient for her that he was there to increase the small circle of people she knew. It could make all the difference to the good time she had at the ball.

George stopped the car near to the open doorway to the sounds of voices as people streamed in. Cars moved off to park at some distance and others took their place. Inside the great hall banked with flowers, chandeliers brought new life to panelled walls adorned by ancient shields, sabres, and claymores forming a constant reminder of feuds and gatherings long since past.

George carried his daughter in, followed by Rob with the wheelchair, with Laraine waiting behind them for Moira to be seated before going forward. Charles was there with the light shining on his blond hair.

Clad in a kilt and black velvet evening jacket, he appeared taller than most of the people around him. Had the ball been held somewhere other than McGreyfarne, Laraine was convinced that he would still unconsciously demand attention. He had the congenital gift of causing people to gravitate to him as though borne along on his magnetic personality and charm.

Quite unexpectedly his head turned to where she was standing. His glance was brief as arriving guests demanded his attention, but it was enough to make the hot colour rush to her face. Hastily she had moved behind Rob and when they moved forward Laraine attempted to recover her composure. Then Charles seemed to have no eyes for anyone but Moira. His gaze travelled over the blonde head, the lines of her face and the very pretty evening dress. He bent over her to murmur something that brought the colour to her cheeks, before greeting Rob and George.

There was no time except for preliminaries and when he greeted her Laraine was able to look at him with a cool composure which she did not feel. Margaret came eagerly to meet them.

Charles, she explained, had insisted on her resting her foot instead of standing with him in the hall to greet the guests. Soon people were bearing down upon them and Laraine was introduced to many of the locals. She noticed that most of the men wore kilts and that the women had an air of modern sophistication. Some of them regarded her with a mild curiosity, but they were cordial.

A Swedish table had been prepared along with an improvised bar.

Waiters glided by bearing trays of drinks and Moira was surrounded by friends anxious to hear the latest news of her disability—was she going to ride again, and so on. Jock and George were soon claimed by their womenfolk and Charles was there lending an ear to an elderly dowager while he paired, separated and introduced guests with an unerring instinct and charm.

When the band started it was a cue for everyone to move into the adjoining ballroom where chairs and tables filled the outer rim for those who did not wish to dance. The dances were a mixture of English and Scottish, and Laraine was immediately claimed by Rob. They frolicked through the Gay Gordons, then went on to more sophisticated dancing.

Laraine was never without partners. She danced several times with George and Rob and was besieged by other young men eager to dance with her. Quite often she spared a glance to look to where Moira sat with Margaret. Most of the time they were blotted out by people talking to them. Apparently Moira's accident had provoked a great deal of interest and sympathy among the community. No doubt there was speculation as to her marriage to Charles.

He had not come near to ask her to dance. At the interval for refreshments he circulated among the guests making sure everyone was enjoying themselves. Moira was talking and laughing with a drink in her hand. Margaret and her father were there when Laraine joined them with Rob. All around remarks about the ball being a success were heard. But then the Hunt Ball was always a success, boomed one voluble elderly lady standing nearby. Frankly, she said, most people loved to dance and she could not imagine anything more horrible than not being able to.

Fortunately her husband bore her away, having seen Moira's face.

'Old faggot!' she murmured.

Laraine agreed with her and silently congratulated Moira on taking it so well. It could not be easy for her to see other young things dancing in the arms of virile young man while she was imprisoned in a wheelchair.

The evening was well under way when Laraine took advantage of an interlude in the dancing to go to see if Moira was beginning to get tired and wanted to go home, but she was halted half way across the room by the sight of Charles joining the little group. Not wishing to intrude, she swung round and made her way quickly back to the ballroom. The next dance had begun and she moved swiftly to the open French windows. Escaping from Charles had unnerved her a little. Really, it was ridiculous the way he had the power to send tremors across her nerves. Besides, it was disloyal to Moira, and Laraine despised herself for it. So far the evening had been wonderful. She liked the people, the lovely countryside, and the slow tempo of living. But somehow Charles spoiled it all for her and it frightened her.

Maybe he was right when he hinted that the job could wear her down. She must be nervous and overwrought, she told herself, to exaggerate his power of attraction—for that was what it was, an exaggeration, a mere clash of personalities.

Silently, deeply she breathed in the cool sweet air perfumed with nocturnal scents from the grounds. Fairy lights among the trees presented a scene of unreality, flowers looked waxen and artificial, and the only movement was of couples strolling out to enjoy the night air.

Suddenly she quivered on a note of warning as a figure materialised at her side.

'May I have the next dance, Laraine?' asked Charles smoothly.

Before she could reply he had drawn her into the room and taken her into his arms. They circled the room and neither of them spoke. She had known that he would dance well, but not that they would be in perfect unison with each other. It was like floating on air and she hoped he would not speak to spoil it. He didn't. They might have been dancing under a spell. The dancers around them were just a blur.

Only when the music stopped did she come back to earth, a little bewildered, a little afraid. She stiffened as he released her.

'Thank you,' he said. 'You are an accomplished dancer.'

She said flippantly, 'Did you watch my performance before you decided to ask me for a dance?'

He bowed mockingly. 'A simple deduction, my child,' he answered sardonically. 'Anyone with the slenderness of a young sapling couldn't help but dance divinely.'

Laraine made no answer. She walked by his side back to where Moira sat. She was with her father, Margaret and Rob.

Margaret said, 'Moira is tired and wants to go home, but you can stay if you like.'

'I would rather go with Moira,' Laraine replied. 'It's been a wonderful evening, and I've enjoyed it very much, thanks.'

Much later in the silence of her room, Laraine lay wide-eyed and sleepless in her bed. The night had been one to remember. Charles had not spoiled it for her after all. Dancing with him had made the evening complete. It had been an evening that she would remember all her life. The magic of being in his arms still lingered, and she hoped rather wistfully that he had felt some of that magic too when he had danced with her. The moment the thought passed through her mind Laraine instantly dismissed it as being unworthy. How mean and despicable could one be in dreaming of a man who already belonged to someone else, and a person who could not fight back? The most sensible thing to do was to forget the evening as though it had never been, treat it as unreal—as unreal as the flowers she had looked at earlier at McGreyfarne in the fairy lights and the moon.

With her head buried beneath the bedclothes, Laraine shut out all thoughts of Charles and eventually slept.

Now that the swimming pool at Lochdoone was completed, Moira's father decided to give a party and invite all her young friends. It was to take place after lunch and go on through the afternoon around the pool, weather permitting. Rob had been invited, but had refused on the excuse of pressure of work. He had to go to town on the morning of the party and would not be back until late. Laraine knew he had work to do before he left at the end of the month, but she felt he was determined not to mix with them socially for some reason. As for Moira, her behaviour went true to pattern, with her off days and long periods of not speaking. Laraine had become used to moods which were no longer embarrassing to her, but it did worry her when for no reason at all Moira began to wheel herself around the grounds. On these occasions she was never far away because of unforeseen accidents with the wheelchair.

Rob had a flat over the stables, and his meals were taken there by Dougal when he was not dining out. A woman came from the village each morning to clean for him. One morning Moira had wheeled herself in that direction and it set Laraine wondering, but she was soon back, alone.

Mindful of what Charles had said about becoming too friendly with Rob, Laraine had not encouraged his advances. There had been times when she had been sorely tempted to be friends because he appeared to be both lonely and unhappy, but always the thought of hurting Moira had held her back. She hoped he was doing the right thing in going abroad, but he certainly did not seem to be very happy about it.

On the day that George had planned the opening of the swimming pool Moira was sitting on the terrace when she suddenly disappeared. She had sent Laraine indoors for their painting gear and Laraine had returned to find her gone. She searched the grounds and as she came within sight of the swimming pool saw the reason for her sudden departure from the terrace. Seeing Rob in the grounds, Moira had given chase and stopped him near to the swimming pool.

Laraine was too far away to hear what was being said, but she saw Rob make an impatient gesture with a brown hand.

Moira's voice rose angrily in reply, then Rob was striding
away past the pool to disappear towards the house. For
several moments Moira, taken aback by his abrupt departure, sat staring after him. Then she called his name,
and wrenched the wheelchair around as though to follow
him. What happened next was most unnerving to Laraine,
who stared with horror as the wheelchair made a half turn,
keeled half over, righted itself and careered madly towards
the swimming pool. The next moment it had toppled over
into the pool. As she ran Laraine heard Rob go off in the
estate car and knew there would be no help coming from
him.

There was no time to do more than slip off her sandals
before plunging in the water. Moira, hampered by her
clothes, was trying to keep afloat when Laraine reached her.
It was the work of seconds to get her back to the side of
the pool.

As she hauled her out she heard Moira give a brief exclamation of pain.

'Did I hurt you?' she asked as they both collapsed pant-
ing on the side of the pool.

Moira pushed soaking wet hair from her face. 'No,' she
gasped. 'Just my leg, that's all.'

'Your leg?' Laraine almost shrieked in her excitement.
'You mean you actually felt your leg?'

Moira shook her head. 'It was nothing. My legs dragged
a bit as you pulled me from the water. How was it you
came so quickly?'

It took several seconds for Laraine to recover from her
disappointment at Moira's reply, and the hope that there
had been some nerve reaction in her legs died. She was
aware of her companion eyeing her warily as she wondered
how much she had seen of her encounter with Rob.

Diplomatically, she said, 'I came in search of you, just in
time to see you topple into the pool.' She laughed, because
they looked very sorry sights indeed with their saturated
clothes clinging to them and their hair like rats' tails. Her

laughter was also a measure of releasing her relief that Moira had suffered nothing worse than a ducking. 'I'd better go for help,' she gurgled. 'We look anything but glamorous!' She peered over the side of the pool and shook her head at the sight of the wheelchair on the bottom. 'We'll need help to get the wheelchair up again. Sure you're all right?'

Moira smiled. 'Yes—and thanks.'

'For what? For fishing you out of the pool? Accidents will happen to the best of people. Stay where you are until I come back. Don't move!'

With this quip, Laraine jumped to her feet and ran towards the house. George was in his study when she burst in, wringing wet with water streaming off her.

'Don't panic,' she gasped. 'Moira and I have been trying out the pool fully dressed and we made the mistake of taking the wheelchair in as well! We're both wringing wet and I think you'd better take a blanket to wrap Moira in or your clothes will be wet when you carry her in.'

Fortunately the air was warm and they were no worse for their wetting.

The party around the pool that afternoon was a happy affair with everyone enjoying themselves. Moira had a surfeit of young men eager to take her into the water, and the fact that all the guests were young contributed to the air of festivities. A long table beneath a canopy had been set alongside the pool with food and drinks with Dougal and his wife taking charge.

Laraine had helped, happy that everything had turned out so well. She was glad that Moira had joined in so wholeheartedly after being so surly about it. Charles had not come because he was away, and Margaret was still resting her injured knee. George was also absent, having gone to McGreyfarne after receiving a telephone call from there after lunch.

Laraine had known that she would miss Charles when she moved to Lochdoone, but she was appalled at how empty her life seemed without his vibrant presence. It was shattering. She might have known him all her life instead of a short time. Laraine told herself that the longer he kept away the better for her in every way. Her feeling for him was something she had to fight, otherwise how would she go on when he had gone out of her life for ever?

Sitting on the edge of the pool, she gazed into the water to see Moira swimming strongly with two young men in tow. Impossible to believe that beneath her façade of gaiety lay the tragedy of paralysed limbs. Against the background of voices reverberating from the water Laraine thought again of Charles. If it were only possible for Moira to get well again! Then she could go away happy that he would live a normal life with a wife and children. Poignantly the thought occurred that he even might look back and remember Laraine Winters with a little affection.

By seven o'clock that evening the last of the guests had gone, leaving Laraine and Moira to make their way indoors. The wheelchair had been taken from the pool and had dried out during the afternoon in the sun. Dougal had polished it up and put on fresh cushions. It was ready when Moira needed it to return indoors.

Laraine was ready for dinner that evening when Moira wheeled herself unexpectedly into her room. She was wearing the velvet skirt and pretty georgette top that Margaret had made for her. Her skin glowed from being out in the sun and there was an air of resignation about her as if she had suddenly come to terms with herself. This was very gratifying to Laraine, who had hitherto regarded her as restless and bitterly unhappy. The fundamental reasons for it had not changed, of course, but somehow the room suddenly assumed a listening quality as though something of importance had happened.

She said sincerely, 'You're looking very pretty. How's the wheelchair, not too damp after being in the water, I hope?'

'It's all right.' At first Moira spoke in her usual offhand fashion, then as she went on her tones warmed. 'I want to talk to you before we go down to dinner. First of all I must thank you for not telling Daddy that it was my own bad temper that was responsible for me falling into the pool this morning. I simply lost control of the chair. You knew that, didn't you? You must have seen me talking to Rob to be on the spot so quickly after I fell in the water.'

'Really?' Laraine sat at the dressing table making her face up lightly, and her eyes met Moira's accusing ones as she drew up in her wheelchair behind her.

Moira bit her lip as if she was finding it difficult to say what she had to. 'You know you did. You made light of the whole thing, treating it as a joke and encouraging others, including my father, to do the same. I'm very grateful.'

'I did nothing. Besides, look at it this way. Falling in the water gave you the confidence to join in the fun this afternoon instead of dithering on the side of the pool. You did enjoy it, didn't you?'

'Yes, I did.' Moira moved uncomfortably in her chair. 'But I wish you wouldn't be so nice about it,' she exclaimed impatiently. 'You make me aware that I have a conscience —which brings me to the next thing I have to tell you. I'm not going to marry Charles.'

Laraine's hand was shaking as she was about to touch her lips with an outliner. The words hit her like shrapnel, giving the same sense of shock.

'But ... but why?' she stammered.

'Let's say I've done a bit of growing up since you came.'

'And that's decided you not to marry Charles. I would have thought it had strengthened your resolve to marry him. Why don't you want to marry him?'

'It wouldn't be right.'

Laraine said gently, 'Surely Charles will have something to say about that. You don't want to hurt him, surely?'

Moira shrugged. 'He'll get over it.'

'You haven't changed your mind about seeing that man in Rome about another check-up, I suppose?'

Laraine lightly made up her lips, gave a brief glance at

her face in the mirror, then turned around for Moira's
reply.

'No, I haven't.'

It was then that Laraine felt that there was nothing more
to say.

CHAPTER TWELVE

GEORGE was pleased to learn that the party at the swimming pool had been a success. He told Laraine so at breakfast the next morning.

With a twinkle in his eye, he said, 'I believe Moira enjoyed herself in the water. At least you would both enjoy it more in your swimsuits than diving in fully clothed. I don't suppose you've managed to change her mind about seeing the specialist in Rome?'

Laraine shook her head. She felt it disloyal to tell him of the conversation with Moira the previous evening. Her decision not to marry Charles was her own business and she must tell her father herself about it. What bothered Laraine was where did they go from here. Was the answer at McGreyfarne? Remembering that he had been visiting there until late the previous evening she asked, 'How is the invalid?'

George appeared to be concentrating more than usual on pouring out the coffee.

'As a matter of fact,' he said at length, 'she's had a fall—nothing serious; it happened when she was out taking Mac for a walk. Apart from grazed hands and a cut knee no great harm was done, but it had shaken her, and Morag telephoned to say that Charles was away. So I went over to spend the day with her.' He passed her cup of coffee with shadowed eyes. 'As a matter of fact she gave me a list of things she had intended to buy in town and I wondered if you would get them for her. You can take the car.'

'I'd be glad to. I'm awfully sorry about Margaret,' said Laraine, and meant it. In the comparatively short time she had spent at McGreyfarne, she had become part of their lives, and had slipped naturally into the pattern of it. To

173

her surprise Moira did not accompany her to town. On tele-
phoning Margaret she had learned that Charles was expected back home at midday, so she decided to go to Mc-
Greyfarne while Laraine was shopping in town. Her father
was to take her there and he could take the shopping that
Laraine brought back from town when he called to take her
back to Lochdoone from McGreyfarne in the evening.

On her way to her room to get ready for her outing to
town, Laraine wondered how Charles would take Moira's
decision not to marry him. It occurred to her then that
Moira had revealed little of her former life; her rift with
Rob, like her life with Charles, was a closed book. Then
there was Margaret. The longing to know more about
where she stood in relation to George had been almost
overpowering at times, but she had resisted the impulse to
ask Moira. Laraine was not the inquisitive type and if at
times she had thought that it would have helped if Moira
had been more forthcoming, she had stifled the thought
since it was obvious that her charge dominated the scene.
Had Rob wanted to marry her? If he had why then was she
so hostile to him? And George? Had Moira put paid to any
romance between himself and Margaret? Upon reflection
Moira was the dominating factor—even with Charles.

Before leaving for town Laraine took the envelope containing the money that Charles had returned so angrily to
her handbag and put it away for safe keeping until such
time as she left. The last thing she was going to do on the
termination of her employment at Lochdoone was to post it
to him.

On the drive to town she revelled in the idyllic stretch of
the countryside, the fresh sweet air and the freedom to roam
and enjoy the absolute peace of nature as yet not ravaged by
man. In the delightful town with its magnificent square and
mellowed Georgian houses backed by the river, she made
her purchases, coloured cottons, fine cobwebby lace, ribbon,
enchanting buttons, and belts. On Margaret's list were a number of other things that would all end up on her workroom.

Laraine wondered sadly how Margaret would take Moira's refusal to marry Charles. Would she see her own dream of happiness with George disappearing for ever? Laraine pulled herself up sharply at this point to find herself at the entrance to the library. One thing she had to remember was that it was not her business to try and solve other people's problems. The thing to remember was that Laraine Winters was just a ship that was passing in the night, nothing more.

In the library she was lucky enough to find the two books Margaret had asked for, and after having lunch she set off for Lochdoone with everything she had been requested to bring. Her heart dipped as a turn in the drive revealed a big familiar car, that of Charles. With a swiftly beating heart Laraine heaped parcels in her arms and walked up the steps into the hall. She was piling them on to the hall table when Jock appeared, to say that she was wanted in the library.

Laraine's nerves tightened as she entered the room to see Charles reclining indolently in one of the big roomy chairs. He rose to his feet as she entered, and so did a rather dapper man who had been sitting opposite to him at the hearth.

Charles said smoothly, 'Laraine, I want you to meet Dottore Benito Padrilli from Rome. Dottore Padrilli, Miss Laraine Winters, who is Miss Frazer's companion. Sit down, Laraine. Dottore Padrilli would like to speak to you.'

Charles gestured to the chair he had vacated and went to lean nonchalantly against the side of the fireplace.

So this was the great man from Rome whom Moira's father had been wanting her to meet! Of medium height, with sleek black hair and liquid dark eyes gleaming with a professional regard, Dottore Padrilli was handsome with the beautiful bone structure of face often to be seen among the Italians. Her eyes fell in sudden confusion as she sat down, for he was smiling and in the dark depths of his eyes a tiny light flickered for a brief moment of admiring appraisal.

'And now, Miss Winters,' he said, after bending low over her hand and reseating himself, 'I wish you to tell me all you have learned about Miss Frazer since you came to be her companion. Everything about her illness that is, this paralysed condition of the legs.'

Laraine moistened her lips, aware of Charles looking down at her, and discovered that facing the barrage of Italian black eyes was preferable to meeting the cynical ones of Charles.

She began, 'There's little to tell really. I haven't seen any sign of life returning in them. While I have at times massaged her shoulders to good effect to relieve any migraine she's had, I was not encouraged to do the same to her legs. Incidentally, I'm not fully qualified in that respect in any case.'

Dottore Padrilli nodded. 'And you are sure there is nothing that you can remember that will help me in any way. Think again, Miss Winters, please.'

Charles cut in at this point, 'Moira is not the best of patients. She's a law unto herself. But she has plenty of courage.'

Laraine glanced at him surreptitiously under her lashes and bit her lip at the sudden tenderness in his face as he spoke. He was evidently very much in love with Moira, she thought. I have to think hard. I have to help him.

At length she said, 'There was one thing. It happened as I was pulling Moira from the swimming pool yesterday. Her legs dragged a little against the side of the pool and I heard her give a small cry of distress.'

'Yes, yes, then what?' The doctor was leaning forward in his chair, arms along his thighs, dark eyes burning into her face as she paused.

Weakly she added, 'I'm afraid that's all. Apparently she felt nothing in her legs other than them being an encumbrance.'

The doctor smiled, looked at her speculatively. 'You have been most helpful, Miss Winters. Would you say that you were in Miss Frazer's confidence?'

Laraine regarded him candidly. 'No, I wasn't. But then I never actually invited it. I think she was against sharing her world with a stranger like myself. There was always this feeling that she had to cling on to a fast-diminishing circle around her.'

Dottore Padrilli inclined his head comprehendingly. 'Too bad you were not a young man,' he answered dryly. 'You might then have gained more of Miss Frazer's confidence. Would you not agree, Charles?'

'Entirely,' Charles answered, coolly, mockingly. 'Instead we have two extremely pretty girls, one of whom is incapacitated.'

'But not for always, we hope,' said the doctor. 'I am most grateful for your help, Miss Winters.' Rising to his feet, he gave her a polite little bow, then addressed Charles. 'You say Miss Frazer is at your home? I suggest we go at once. You have no objection to my examining her there?'

Quite decisively, Charles said, 'Of course not. The sooner the better.'

With a nod to Laraine he strolled with the doctor to the door of the room. It was then that Laraine remembered the parcels on the hall table. Running after Charles, she caught his sleeve.

'I've been doing some shopping for your aunt,' she said with a slight rise of colour at his uplifted brows. 'The parcels are on the hall table. Will you take them with you?'

'Certainly,' he answered, adding with a tight mocking smile, 'Do we owe you any money?'

She stiffened, seeing him reach automatically for his wallet, and gave a pale smile. 'No. Your aunt had an account at the shops I visited.'

The doctor had opened the library door and Charles flicked a glance across the hall to the pile of parcels on the hall table. An attractive eyebrow was lifted queryingly at the bouquet of flowers by the parcels.

'And the flowers?' he asked.

'A gift from me to your aunt with my love,' Laraine answered evenly.

He looked down at her for several seconds as though about to say something, then changed his mind and strode across the hall after the doctor. Together they gathered up the parcels and the flowers and went out to the car.

By the time Laraine reached her room she was wondering whether the information she had given to Dottore Padrilli about Moira was of any significance. She hoped from the bottom of her heart that it was. Meanwhile she had the afternoon to herself, and what better than to spend it in the swimming pool?

Rob met her in the hall as she returned fresh and sparkling from a swim in the pool. He looked tired and jaded.

'Any chance of a cup of tea?' he asked. 'I've just finished work, and I felt in need of company. I saw you down at the pool.'

Laraine smiled warmly. 'If I know Mrs Dougal tea will be waiting for me in the lounge! Give me five minutes to change and I'll be down.'

Swiftly she fled to her room, changed into a pastel pink trouser suit in cool cotton, combed her hair, and not bothering to put on make-up, went down to join Rob. Sure enough Mrs Dougal had been in with the tea tray. There it was on a small table and Rob was standing staring out of the window into the grounds.

'I suppose you'll miss all this,' Laraine remarked as she poured out the tea.

Slowly he strolled to a chair, lowered himself into it and accepted the cup of tea she offered.

'There'll be other places, I suppose,' he said. 'How come you aren't at McGreyfarne with Moira?'

She told him as he thirstily drank down most of the tea. She also told him about Charles' visit with Dottore Padrilli. Rob did not exclaim in surprise as she expected. Instead he finished the rest of his tea and proffered the cup to be refilled.

'Poor Moira,' he said at length. 'It was rotten luck for the accident to happen. Did the great man hold out any hope of her walking again?'

Laraine passed him a refill. 'He didn't say, but I have a feeling that he was confident enough.'

She cut a generous portion of Mrs Dougal's fruit cake for Rob and passed it to him on a plate, then cut a much smaller piece for herself. Normally her appetite would be sharpened by swimming in the pool, but this afternoon it remained dormant. There was a peculiar feeling of some crisis or other in the offing.

Rob demolished a portion of his cake, then asked casually, 'Did you know that Doctor Padrilli was coming here?'

'No. Could be that Moira's father decided to invite him as a last resort. After all, she did refuse to see the man.'

Rob did not agree. 'There's more to it than that. After I'd finished work this afternoon I called at my place before coming on here. There was a message for me from Margaret to say that you and I have been invited to dinner there this evening. Nothing more.'

Laraine felt all feeling drain from her. 'Do you mind if I don't go with you?'

'Not go? Why not? Surely you want to know what the great man says about Moira's chances of walking again?'

'That's just the point. You see, I've always been so optimistic about Moira walking again. Now I'm scared. What if she still refuses to let the doctor examine her? Worse still, what if she does, and he doesn't give much hope?'

'In that case she'll need you to comfort her.'

Laraine shook her head sadly. 'Only someone close to her can do that.' She thought of Charles and dismissed him with a tremor. 'Someone she loves.'

Rob pushed the plate with the rest of his cake away from him as if he had lost any desire for it, and drank the rest of his tea.

'Sure you won't go with me this evening?' he asked morosely.

Laraine shook her head and said contritely, 'Sorry. Won't you finish your cake, and have some more tea? There's plenty in the pot.'

He gestured the offer away. 'What excuse must I make for you?'

'Say I have a headache.'

The excuse was not without foundation, because already her head was feeling tight and tense. Headaches were not usually something she suffered from, but she had experienced several since coming to Lochdoone.

Rob stared intently at her pallor, the shadows around her eyes, her vulnerable look which, had she but known it, endeared her to him. His lips moved as though about to say something, then he rose heavily to his feet.

'I must push off,' he said. 'I've some letters to write before this evening. I suppose I'd better turn up at McGreyfarne in case they think you and I have eloped.' Suddenly he bent forward with both hands planted firmly on the table, palms upwards. His face was very near to hers and he grinned. 'What about it, Laraine? I shall need a wife where I'm going!'

She laughed, bent forward and kissed the tip of his nose. 'Get away with you! You'll find a wife easily enough, someone who'll love you as you deserve to be loved.'

Her emotions mixed, Laraine went to her room thankful for an evening on her own. On her way she met Mrs Dougal and explained that she would not be going out that evening and would like a tray sent up to her room instead of dining on her own downstairs. Too restless to settle, Laraine did a few chores, washed her hair, then putting on a wrap, curled up in a chair with a book until supper time.

Her head felt much clearer, but there was still a strange feeling of expectancy keeping her senses for ever on the alert. Every sound in the house seemed to her strained ears to be amplified and she started with a sudden palpitation when Dougal tapped on her door.

She was wanted on the telephone. It was Margaret, enquiring if she was feeling any better and expressing her disappointment at not seeing her. She thanked her for doing her shopping so beautifully and also for the lovely gift of the flowers. She made light of her recent fall and was feeling fine again herself. After saying she hoped to see Laraine soon, she said someone else was waiting to speak to her.

It was Dottore Padrilli. 'Good news, Miss Winters,' he announced. 'I've examined Miss Frazer and slight bruises on her shins bear out what you said about her giving a cry of pain when you pulled her from the swimming pool. Part of the reason for her paralysis is psychological, the need to keep an adoring circle of friends around her by remaining helpless. We have a long way to go, but I am very hopeful of the outcome.'

Laraine said breathlessly, 'You mean she actually allowed you to examine her?'

'Love is a very powerful force, Miss Winters. After I had examined Miss Frazer she refused to go to Rome for treatment, and that was where love stepped in. She is going to Rome with her fiancé. Later, they plan to marry there. I shall be leaving early in the morning, so I will say goodbye. If you should ever come to Rome do call to see me. I would be so very happy to show you around our lovely city. Goodbye, Miss Winters.'

Laraine put down the receiver on a sense of shock. She could not believe it. Moira was going to walk again. Tears rolled down her face. She played a part in her final recovery after all. Charles too—one could say it had been a combined operation. And now he was going to marry the girl he loved. He had obviously ruled out her decision not to marry him—his potent charm would not have to be stretched to the limit to do that. Now there was nothing for her to do except pack her case and leave.

It would hurt to leave, but that was nothing to feel wretched about. She had come with a purpose in mind and now that purpose was fulfilled. The fact that it had cost her dear because she had been foolish enough to fall in love with Charles did not matter—must not matter. There would be other jobs, and a change of scene could work wonders.

Dougal brought her supper and she ate it mechanically. When Dougal came for the tray she was feeling more normal. To her surprise he said that she was wanted downstairs in the main lounge.

'A party from McGreyfarne,' was how he put it.

Hastily Laraine shed her wrap, grabbed the first dress to hand in her wardrobe, and hastily made herself presentable. She left her newly washed hair to chance, flicking it to curl naturally around her face. Her make-up was sketchy, a hastily applied powder puff and a touch of lipstick. Breathless by the time she reached the lounge, Laraine paused outside the door long enough to compose herself, then entered the room.

'Good evening, Laraine,' Charles said sardonically. 'I trust you're feeling better?'

Her face went white, then flooded with colour. 'My headache ... er ... it's much better,' she stammered. 'But I don't understand ... Dougal said ...'

'A party from McGreyfarne?' he finished for her. 'My words exactly, I'm afraid.'

Laraine clenched her hands in an effort to stop her trembling.

'That wasn't very funny,' she cried indignantly.

'It wasn't meant to be. I'm sorry I had to use the expression in case you had cold feet again.'

She lifted her chin and glared at him. 'What do you mean by that?'

'You were afraid to come to McGreyfarne, as you're now afraid to be alone with me in this room.' He strolled towards her lazily. 'Do come in and close the door.'

Laraine had teetered in the doorway at the sight of him and he gently drew her inside, leading her across to a chair with fingers like steel cupping her elbow.

'I don't know what you hope to gain from this visit,' Laraine began after putting the chair between them and clutching the back. 'Will you please say what you have to say, then go. I ... I need hardly tell you that Dottore Padrilli has told me everything that has happened.'

'Not everything,' he replied, sitting down on the arm of the chair and looking straight at her.' The most important event of the evening to me, apart from the good news about Moira, is about to happen now. You would have heard it at McGreyfarne if you hadn't had cold feet.'

Laraine clenched the back of the chair with white knuckles. 'If you say that again, I'll ... I'll ...' She broke off, trembling.

'Slap my face?' The idea of her hitting him amused him, and his hands suddenly held hers prisoner on the back of the chair. 'Why not kiss me instead?'

Futilely Laraine tried to free her hands from his remorseless grip and failed. Charles was laughing at her and her anger did much to steady her.

'How dare you taunt me like this!' she cried. 'I ... I know how deliriously happy you must feel about everything, but ... but ... I can't for the life of me see why you should come here and behave like this. I can only think that you must be drunk, or something.'

'Could be,' he admitted smoothly. 'I have had two glasses of champagne on an empty stomach before coming here.'

'If you missed your dinner it must have been your own fault.'

'Yours as well, since you refused to come to McGreyfarne. I've come to take you back to join in the celebrations.'

'You've what?' Vainly Laraine strove not to succumb to the fire running through her veins from their clasping hands. White to the lips, she said,

'How can you talk like that? It's Moira's evening and yours. Can't you see that?'

When he shook his head she rushed on. 'I can guess what you're thinking—that I shall feel left out if I'm not there this evening. But it isn't so. I do hope you'll both be very happy.'

'Thanks. I have no doubt about that. However, I've brought a bottle of champagne with me, so let's have a drink, shall we?'

Charles released her hands, rose to his feet, and strode to a table containing a bottle of champagne and glasses. Releasing the cork with a sharp plop, he poured out two glasses, and gave her one. Laraine came from behind the chair to take hers with a worried frown.

'Should you drink more on an empty stomach?' she asked weakly. 'After all, you have to drive back to McGreyfarne.'

He grinned whitely, and she looked at him in some alarm. If he was slightly tipsy there was no doubt that he was acting completely out of character, but she had to bear with him. Much had happened to account for it.

He lifted his glass. 'To Moira and her complete recovery.'

They drank. Then he said, 'To Moira and Rob.'

They drank again, and if Laraine had any previous doubts about him being drunk his final toast convinced her.

'To us,' he said.

She emptied her glass and allowed him to take it from her trembling fingers. The champagne had done much in helping her to recover from the shock of seeing Charles again. How she loved him! It was not fair that she had to go through this torment. But love is akin to compassion and she wanted so much to draw his head against her and tell him that she understood.

'Another drink?' He looked at her strangely, and when she shook her head added, 'If the shock of seeing me meant what I think it did just now then it makes it much easier to tell you that I love you.'

Laraine went white. That he could stand there and declare his love for her after the way he had treated her was beyond understanding. But there were no scathing words, no bitterness in her reply, only weary disbelief.

'I ... I realise the strain you've been under, but I don't think I can take any more from you.'

His reaction was startling. His eyes blazed. He raked a hand through the blond hair and glared at her.

'Hell,' he roared, 'I can't take much more myself either!'

The next moment he lunged towards her, hauled her into his arms and claimed her mouth with his own. His actions were so swift, so unexpected, that any resistance on her part was swamped by the wonder and ecstasy of being in his arms. All resistance fled, leaving only complete and utter surrender to an agonizing joy.

He was all fire and passion, carrying her along with him and showing her all that life meant of love, joy and beauty. When he lifted his head he gave her no chance to speak before he began to kiss her again. Laraine could only hang on until the warm response of her sweet trembling mouth brought about a wonderful tenderness in him. Gradually his cruel grip slackened and he released her enough to gaze down at the pale glow of her face raised to his. His eyes rested upon her mouth lovely from his kisses, and a slow smile lifted the corners of his lips.

Absolutely beyond words, Laraine could only stare up at him wide-eyed and bewildered. No longer was he cynical and arrogant. He was visibly moved, almost humble. To her it was frightening. He took her hands and kissed them gently.

'I was right in daring to think that you loved me. You have to. I've always loved you from our first meeting at the railway station that day. You hit me right between the eyes and I've not been the same since. But you see, my sweet, I'd never been in love before, and I resented being taken over by a force stronger than myself. So I fought against it, but I lost.'

'But Moira?' she asked dazedly, curling her fingers around his.

He groaned and drew her against him to rest his chin on her hair.

He said, 'I was never in love with Moira. I was sorry for her, so I allowed a combination of circumstances to draw us together. You must remember that I hadn't met you then.

Besides, her accident was also a tragedy for George and my aunt Margaret. They've been in love for years, but Aunt Margaret wouldn't marry him until Moira was no longer his responsibility—in short, until she married.'

He hugged her tightly, kissed her hair and continued, 'I'm not saying that I might not have married Moira eventually. I'd never met a girl I'd wanted to marry then. I'd never known what love was until I met you and my own small private hell began. You were everything I'd looked for in a woman, demure, feminine, good company, with your lovely eyes filled with compassion for a poor little hedgehog and a girl in a wheelchair. I loved your sense of humour, your courage, your understanding and tolerance of human frailty, your fierce devotion to a case for which there seemed to be little hope. I loved everything about you. Can you wonder that I was terrified of losing you? It was shattering. Here I was loving you to distraction and resenting you at the same time.' He kissed her gently. 'I'm sorry I was so beastly to you. I wasn't myself, and I won't be until we're married.'

Once again he was all fire and passion convincing her of his love by his consuming kisses. And Laraine swooned in the delicious sensation of returning them. It was some time before Charles put her from him and told her to fetch a wrap for their drive back to McGreyfarne.

'Now, this minute?' she gasped, breath regained. 'But you said something about having champagne on an empty stomach. Is it wise to drive without having eaten? Perhaps Mrs Dougal will fix you a sandwich ...'

His eyes teased. 'You'll be safe enough with me, my sweet. At least I hope so—but not in the way you mean. We shall probably keep stopping on the way to convince ourselves that we belong together at last. In any case, dinner has been put back until we arrive back at McGreyfarne.'

He laughed, all fire and sparkle with a look in his eyes which made her run for her wrap in confusion. As he said, they stopped on the way, and those brief ecstatic moments passed all too quickly. His passion flowed over her like drugged wine. His kisses left her dazed and shaken. Trembling in the sweet darkness, she spoke urgently against his lips.

'I think we'd better go, don't you?'

'Why?'

'Because I'm beginning to understand what you meant just now about my being safe with you. You see, I love you, Charles.'

There was a short silence, then he said quietly, 'Say that again.'

'I love you, Charles. Like you, I fought against it and lost.'

She leaned forward then to kiss him and laid her head on his shoulder as he started the car.

The hall at McGreyfarne greeted them with a golden warmth. So did everyone there. Laraine thought the late meal was more of a celebration for engaged couples than for Dottore Padrilli. Spirits soared, laughter echoed, glasses clicked.

There were Moira and Rob radiant in their reunion and love—George minus his harassed air, looking years younger, Margaret holding his hand in an aura of quiet happiness, Charles with the look of a lover, and Dottore Padrilli beaming upon them all while keeping a professional eye on his future patient.

When the party broke up in the small hours, Charles held Laraine back. His fingers were on her wrist, closing around her watch.

'Tomorrow we drive into town for your rings and for a wristwatch. This one will have our names inside. You can give Harvey's away. You belong to me now. We can be married almost at once. Aunt Margaret has made most of your trousseau, the rest you can buy in town. You will marry me soon, won't you?'

He tilted back her head with gentle fingers to look deeply into her eyes. In his ardent gaze was all the promise, wonder and frightening delight of what marriage to him would mean.

She smiled. 'As soon as you wish.'

Slowly she reached up to push her fingers through the short tight curls of his blond hair, and added tremulously, 'I'll never forget that first day I met you wearing your blue tartan tam.'

Her laugh was one of pure happiness.

He frowned. 'Was I so funny?'

'You looked delicious.' Laraine hurried on at his look of disgust. 'I can't wait to see our son strutting around in one.'

He was all fire now, his hard cheek against hers, his mouth seeking her trembling one in a sweet caress. Ardent minutes passed.

'What if it's a girl?' he murmured.

'We'll have others,' she said. 'The rafters of McGreyfarne are going to ring with their laughter.'

'Our laughter too, my sweet,' he promised, and his kiss was the most exquisite thing Laraine had ever known.

Harlequin

COLLECTION
EDITIONS OF 1978

**50 great stories
of special beauty
and significance**

$1.25
each novel

In 1976 we introduced the first 100 Harlequin Collections—a selection of titles chosen from our best sellers of the past 20 years. This series, a trip down memory lane, proved how great romantic fiction can be timeless and appealing from generation to generation. The theme of love and romance is eternal, and, when placed in the hands of talented, creative, authors whose true gift lies in their ability to write from the heart, the stories reach a special level of brilliance that the passage of time cannot dim. Like a treasured heirloom, an antique of superb craftsmanship, a beautiful gift from someone loved—these stories too, have a special significance that transcends the ordinary. **$1.25 each novel**

Here are your 1978
Harlequin Collection Editions...

Original Harlequin Romance numbers in brackets

ORDER FORM
Harlequin Reader Service

In U.S.A.
MPO Box 707
Niagara Falls, N.Y. 14302

In Canada
649 Ontario St.,
Stratford, Ontario, N5A 6W2

Please send me the following Harlequin Collection novels. I am enclosing my check or money order for $1.25 for each novel ordered, plus 25¢ to cover postage and handling.

☐ 102	☐ 115	☐ 128	☐ 140
☐ 103	☐ 116	☐ 129	☐ 141
☐ 104	☐ 117	☐ 130	☐ 142
☐ 105	☐ 118	☐ 131	☐ 143
☐ 106	☐ 119	☐ 132	☐ 144
☐ 107	☐ 120	☐ 133	☐ 145
☐ 108	☐ 121	☐ 134	☐ 146
☐ 109	☐ 122	☐ 135	☐ 147
☐ 110	☐ 123	☐ 136	☐ 148
☐ 111	☐ 124	☐ 137	☐ 149
☐ 112	☐ 125	☐ 138	☐ 150
☐ 113	☐ 126	☐ 139	☐ 151
☐ 114	☐ 127		

Number of novels checked @
$1.25 each = $ _____

N.Y. and N.J. residents add
appropriate sales tax $ _____

Postage and handling $ ____.25

TOTAL $ _____

NAME _____

ADDRESS _____
(Please Print)

CITY _____

STATE/PROV. _____

ZIP/POSTAL CODE _____

ROM 2212

A

Offer expires December 31, 1978

And there's still *more* love in

Harlequin
Presents...

Yes!

Four more spellbinding
romantic stories every month
by your favorite authors.
Elegant and sophisticated tales of
love and love's conflicts.

Let your imagination be swept away to
exotic places in search of adventure,
intrigue and romance. Get to
know the warm, true-to-life
characters. Share the special
kind of miracle that
love can be.

Don't miss out. Buy now and discover
the world of HARLEQUIN PRESENTS...

Do you have a favorite
Harlequin author?
Then here is an
opportunity you must
not miss!

HARLEQUIN OMNIBUS

Each volume contains
3 full-length compelling
romances by one author.
Almost 600 pages of
the very best in romantic
fiction for only $2.75

A wonderful way to collect
the novels by the Harlequin
writers you love best!